When The Drummer Falls

by

Spencer Kope

WHEN THE DRUMMER FALLS

FIRST PRINTING

ALL RIGHTS RESERVED
COPYRIGHT © 1995

ISBN 0-9647183-0-8

Library of Congress Catalog Number: 95-90499

Willow Creek Press
Annapolis, Maryland

Dedication

*To those who wore
the Blue and the Gray,
May they rest in Peace*

A Letter Home

June 29, 1863

Dear Mother,

How are you getting on since Father's passing? I hope all is well and you are not too overcome with grief. I pray that I will soon be at your side. This Monday morning finds us marching north to Pennsylvania and Captain Stowe has assured me a discharge when we arrive at Harrisburg.

There's a rumor that we're making for Gettysburgh and I hope in all my heart this is true. I remember the few times Father and I visited there and look forward to seeing it again. I wonder if that little hat shop is still along the main street, near the square. I don't remember its name, but we bought your blue Sunday hat there, remember? If it's still there, I'll maybe stop and have a look.

The men are eager for a scrap with the Rebs. The 83rd is in fine spirits and it would make you terribly proud to see us coming. General Meade has replaced Hooker as Commander of the Army of the Potomac, did you know that? President Lincoln appointed him on Saturday.

The drum you sent is magnificent and I hope you'll give my regards to all who contributed to its purchase. It's the only brass drum in the entire brigade and the other drummers are wonderfully envious.

I must close at this time, we're on the move again. Seems lately we spend most our time marching, so much so that I almost welcome a good fight so as I can rest my feet a spell. Please don't be griev'n too heavily for Father, he's in a better place than you or I. I'll be writing soon.

Your devoted son,

Joshua Harding

1

Ed Williams' Civil War Emporium on Steinwehr Avenue, Gettysburg, Pennsylvania, was a delicate cross between an antique store, a flea market, and a discount outlet for cheap Civil War knock-offs. Knock-offs imported from China, Singapore, the Philippines and a host of other countries competing in the global marketplace for their fair share of the almighty American dollar.

Ed sold everything: Civil War bullets, Rebel and Yankee uniforms – both authentic and reproduced – books, guns, hats, medals, and buckles. Anything and everything the aspiring re-enactor or Civil War buff would want or need. And, of course, Ed Williams had a Union drum.

It was a reproduction drum spewed out of some factory in Taiwan. Perhaps it was because of this faux history that it sat alone and almost forgotten on an upper shelf in the back of the cluttered store.

The dust scattered lightly across its white top told a tale of woeful neglect. And yet it was a drum that yearned to be played, to feel the massage of drum sticks tickling its face, to boisterously shout its *brump rump rump* for all the world to hear. If drums could only dream, that is what the little Taiwanese drum would dream. But no one wanted a dusty old drum from a far away island. Not even Mr. Williams.

Ed was an import himself. Not to the United States, but to Gettysburg. Californian by birth, Ed was Pennsylvanian by choice. After fighting for his country in Korea and winning the Purple Heart for a leg wound that still troubled him on cold Pennsylvania nights, Ed wandered the land. From one town to another. From one job to another. He was searching for himself. Searching for that part of his soul that still haunted the bloody fields of Korea with the souls of his dead friends.

He found it in Gettysburg.

It was the summer of 1958 when the bus pulled into the small Pennsylvania town. Ed's ticket said Harrisburg and he almost didn't get off the bus at Gettysburg as the other passengers filed stiffly down the steps and out the folding door.

The driver said they would only be there fifteen minutes, just long enough to stretch the legs. Ed needed a good leg-stretching, but he needed sleep more. Curling up in his seat, he tried wiggling into a more comfortable position. Only for a second did his eyes fall on the battlefield . . . but that was all it took.

If a picture is worth a thousand words, Gettysburg spoke volumes. The images that greeted this young man as he stared at the battlefield through the dusty window of a wayward bus told a story that seemed to go on forever.

A thousand images danced together on these fields and hills. A million words.

And as he looked, something tugged at the corner of Ed's soul. It pulled him like a rag doll from the seat of that bus and pushed him out onto the gravel-strewn roadway next to the battlefield. A voice from the darkest alcove of his mind seemed to whisper a gentle 'Welcome Home' as his feet stepped lightly onto the rich Pennsylvania soil.

They died here, Ed remembered thinking.

By the thousands they died.

Whether Yank or Reb, they were all Americans. They were warriors like him. In a trance, he walked out onto the battlefield, his hands brushing lightly over the monuments as his fingers traced over the words chiseled deep in the stone. Words meant to honor the brave dead, to bring glory to a terrible invention we call war.

Holy words for an unholy event.

Here were his comrades-in-arms. No matter that they died a hundred years before. They were warriors and Ed Williams honored them with that part of his soul that had been torn from him in Korea.

In time he would discover that he was not alone. Others had come to Gettysburg, searching for themselves and finding instead the dead bones of their ancestors. They were the brethren of war and to them the battlefield was more than history, it was a holy shrine.

Twenty minutes later, as the passengers climbed aboard the bus for the last leg of their journey, Ed knelt next to the scroll-like monument marking the spot where General Armistead fell during Pickett's Charge.

The bus driver honked twice, but Ed didn't move.

There was a strange power, a silent aura about the battlefield.

"What a terrible waste," Ed whispered.

As he stared at the inscription on Armistead's monument, the faces of long dead friends flashed before his eyes. Grim faces that stared at him from the muddy fields of Korea; from eyes that no longer looked upon the mortal world.

If it's true that Death rides a pale horse, Ed thought, *then it is a bloody hoofprint that he has left here in Gettysburg.*

Bowing his head low, Ed Williams hid his face as a tear trickled gently down his cheek. A tear for his fallen comrades.

He would cry only twice in his adult life.

This was the first.

After honking again and getting no response, the bus driver unlocked the luggage compartment and set Ed's two suitcases at the side of the road. Then, in a cloud of carbon monoxide, the driver pulled back onto the road and headed north to Harrisburg. A town that Ed would never visit.

With a solemn certainty he looked upon the small Pennsylvania town and knew that he was home. Home at last.

Ten thousand miles from the horrors of Korea, Ed Williams found peace on the battlefields of Gettysburg.

2

Holding a shattered fragment of metal in his left hand, Ed Williams flipped on his magnification light while his right hand gently, almost invisibly, nudged his bifocals to the tip of his nose.

"Damn eyes," he muttered.

Turning the heavy chunk of metal sideways, then upside down in the light, he scrutinized it carefully. With a paintbrush he dusted some of the dirt from the side of the piece.

"Well," he mused, "it's definitely a six pounder. Can't see any markings on it, though." Lowering the shot fragment, he set it on the counter next to a mixed pile of Confederate and Union bullets.

Andy watched Mr. Williams' face from the other side of the counter, studying the proprietor's wrinkled forehead as the old man crunched the numbers.

"Okay, let's see. Fourteen bullets at the usual rate comes to seven dollars. How 'bout . . . two dollars for the six pounder?"

Andy grimaced the way he always did when he and Mr. Williams played this game. "It's a nice piece, Mr. Williams. I could get at least five for it over at Mr. Estee's."

"All right, four dollars. My final offer."

Andy flashed him a toothy smile. "Deal!"

"What are you boys up to this morning?" Ed asked as he fished in the register drawer for a five and six ones.

"Movie," Andy replied.

Ed looked up, peering down his nose at Andy. The bifocals made his eyes look larger than they really were, almost cartoonish.

"Always with the movies," the old man said. "What is it about you boys and your movies? Every Saturday it's the same thing."

"I bet you went to movies when you were a kid!" Andy said.

"Sure we did. But they didn't cost four seventy-five back then. And popcorn didn't cost two and a half bucks. Besides, when I was growing up we didn't have television. A movie was a treat. Something special."

"Still is," Andy said with a grin. "We like movies."

"Well, there are more important things in life than movies. Especially considering that rubbish you boys watch. You should spend your time more . . . ah, geez! Listen to me will you. Sixty years old and I'm finally sounding like my father."

Handing the money across the counter, Mr. Williams said, "There you are, Sir. Eleven dollars. Have a ball."

"Thanks, Mr. Williams. I'll stop by tonight and help you close if you want."

"I'd like that."

Flashing the old man a smile, Andy headed for the door.

"See you later," he said.

"Count on it," Ed said, smiling as the door closed behind the boy.

*   *   *

They called themselves the Marauders.

Four seventh-graders with mountain bikes and attitude. One was a genius. One, a tough guy. Another told tales that would put Homer to shame, and the last was a hormone in sneakers with three chest hairs and a cracking voice.

Andrew Martin was a native of Gettysburg. Preferring history to the jock-sports of football and baseball, he was in his element on the battlefield. Often, on the steamy afternoons of a Pennsylvania summer, he would pause next to a group of curious tourists as they roamed the battlefield.

These casual historians puzzled the young Andrew Martin as they poured over their maps and books, trying to understand what happened here over a hundred years before.

With the patience of a scribe, Andy would point out McPherson's Woods, Cemetery Ridge, Little Round Top, the Peach Orchard, or any of a dozen other sites, lecturing confidently on the finer points of the three-day conflict.

He did this out of passion, not pride. Andy never bragged and never went out of his way to look smart. But history was his passion and, like his father, he took the subject quite seriously. When he was six – a very precocious six – he decided to follow in his father's footsteps and become a professor of history. It was a decision he held to with steadfast determination.

Matt Jacobs was Andy's best friend, had been since the first grade when Matt moved to Gettysburg from Montana. Matt's dad, a Park Ranger, bought the Pilser's house next door to the Martin's and Andy was waiting to introduce himself the day they moved in.

Living next door to each other, Andy and Matt become fast friends and remained so in the years to come. A genius and a tough guy. It was the perfect recipe for middle school survival.

Grant Woodrow Wilson was the polished and disciplined grandson of a World War II veteran who served as one of the first black paratroopers. Like his Grandpap Wilson, Grant wanted to be a paratrooper. The only problem was his mortal fear of heights.

To him, an escalator was a death chute.

He was a good storyteller though.

On those nights when boredom threatened the Marauder's often boisterous conversations, Grant would spin great tales about Grandpap Wilson's wartime exploits.

Incredible stories about capturing Hitler, only to have him escape by blimp across the Alps. Or racing through France on a stolen Nazi motorcycle with nothing but an M-1 rifle and a throwing knife.

When the boys would corner Grandpap Wilson and ask him if it was so, the old paratrooper would just nod and flash them his toothless grin. "Yep, I remember it well," he'd say, and that would always settle the issue.

Old war heroes never lie.

Jeff Kowalski was the walking hormone, the fourth and final member of the Marauders. He had a thing for any girl or woman with a curve; but in particular, Jeff had a thing for movie star Geena Davis.

He clipped every photo of Geena he came across, plastering them to the walls and ceiling of his bedroom until his mother objected and forced him to stop. Fort Apache, the tree fort in his backyard, now played shrine to his silver screen goddess.

In a world that often seemed too complicated or confused, the Marauders knew exactly were they stood and who they could count on. They were brothers in spirit and with teenage arrogance they claimed to know what life was about and what happiness meant.

But the ever-wise Marauders drew their understanding from lives that were too short to fully comprehend such things. They believed in tangibles and they thought they knew where they were going. They thought they had all the answers.

Most boys do.

But that was before the summer of '94.

3

The carpet-muffled footsteps paused outside Andy's door as they did every night. Paused, but only for a moment, as if to confirm that there was indeed a son in the Martin household and that he did indeed occupy that room. They never entered, just paused in the hall for reassurance. After a moment, the footsteps continued down the hall, only to pause again in front of Brett's room, Andy's younger brother.

Convinced that they were parents – and had been for over a decade – Richard and Alice Martin walked to the end of the hall and closed their bedroom door behind them. The television clicked on as it always did, the barely audible laughter of a late night comedy show seeping through the door and down the hall.

When he was sure they were down for the night, Andy threw his covers off and jumped out of bed, fully clothed and ready to go. Glancing quickly at the clock, he noted the time: ten-thirty.

He was late.

Slipping his backpack out from under the bed, he shoved his arms through the straps and pulled it up high on his back. Next, he unlocked his second story window and eased it up gently. Kneeling, he quickly uncovered what looked like a winch resting against the wall under the window. Unwinding a section of rope ladder from the winch, he tossed it out the window. With the fluid motion brought on by repetition, he quickly fastened a two-foot wide roller to a bracket on the bottom of the window sill.

Grabbing a modified garage door opener off his desk, he pressed it once. Instantly, the rope ladder began to lower itself to the ground, uncoiled by the whisper-quiet motor of the homemade winch. When the ladder was fully extended, it stopped.

Stuffing his pillow under the bedspread for effect, Andy swung first one leg, then the other, out the window and onto the rope ladder. Taking two steps down, he reached up and pulled the window shut as far as it would go.

"Hey!" hissed a voice nearby.

Andy nearly fell off the ladder.

"Where ya going?" the voice demanded with silent urgency.

Looking to his right, Andy could see Brett hanging halfway out his window and shaking his head.

"Where ya going?" Brett repeated.

"None of your bee's wax," Andy snapped.

"I'm gonna tell Mom!" Brett warned.

"You wouldn't."

"Would too!"

Andy sighed. "I'm going to meet the guys."

"Can I go?"

"No!"

"I'll tell."

"No you won't. I'll pound you if you do."

"Ooooo," Brett moaned, holding his hands up to his face and wiggling his fingers. "I'm so scared."

"Come over here and say that," Andy said, waving a fist at his little brother.

Dropping his hands, Brett pleaded, "Come on. You gotta let me go."

Andy shook his head. "Next time."

"Liar. I'm gonna tell." Cocking his head toward the window, Brett cried, "Mom!" eyeing his big brother the whole while.

"Shhh!" Andy hissed.

"Mom!" Brett called again, louder this time.

"All right, you little tattletale," Andy fumed. "I'll take you to the movies tomorrow. Deal?"

"With a big popcorn and a drink," Brett demanded.

"No!"

"Mom!" Brett called again.

"All right! One popcorn and a drink."

"A big popcorn."

"Right! A big popcorn and a drink. Now get back inside and keep your big mouth shut."

Brett shot him a grin and ducked back into his room. A moment later he stuck his head out again. "Happy hunting," he said. Then he was gone.

"Thanks," Andy muttered. "I'm already ten dollars in the hole."

Reaching the bottom of the ladder, he pointed the remote up to a sensor on the roller bar and clicked once. The ladder started back up the side of the house. When it was just below the window sill, Andy clicked the remote again and it stopped.

Smiling, he hid the remote under one of his mom's rosebushes and darted around to the front of the house, to the garage where his bike was parked.

* * *

"You're late!" Jeff barked as Andy locked up his rear tire and slid to a halt next to Matt.

"Shhh! Keep it down!" Andy shot back, glancing anxiously at the sleepy homes lining Sunset Avenue. "Are we ready? Where's Grant?"

"He had to whiz," Jeff said. "Hey, Grant! Hurry up, will ya."

15

"I'm going, I'm going," Grant hissed from the shadow of a large oak in the middle of someone's lawn.

"You're flooding those people's grass," Jeff yelled. "Tie a knot in it and let's go."

As Grant opened his mouth to respond, the porch light clicked on, casting luminous rays across the large front lawn and vaporizing the shadows hiding his very personal endeavor.

"Holy cow!" Grant squealed. Stumbling back from the tree he dropped everything, literally, and bolted across the yard, spraying his pants and shoes while trying to zip himself up. Tripping over an in-ground sprinkler with a remarkable stealth capability, Grant plunged to the ground, slamming nose-first into the hard turf.

Blood oozed.

Grant screamed.

Jumping to his feet, he staggered to the sidewalk, cupping his bloody nose in both hands.

"Hurry up!" Andy said, grabbing Grant by the arm and helping him to his bike. Jeff and Matt were already turning onto King Street and pedaling for their lives toward the Park. Turning south on Steinwehr Avenue, just two blocks from the Civil War Emporium, Andy and Grant raced to catch up. A block later Steinwehr turned into Emmitsburg Road, quickly leaving the town of Gettysburg behind. Like a dark river it carried the boys out into the misty fields and hills that were so very bloody that long ago summer of 1863.

Turning left onto Wheatfield Road, the Marauders pedaled another mile before finally stopping where Crawford Avenue branched off to the right. Dismounting, they walked their bikes over the slotted cattle guard. Devil's Den was just a short ride ahead.

One peculiar thing about thirteen-year old boys, well, boys in general, is that they cannot – *must not* – be taken for cowards.

Oh, they'll run like rabbits when they're scared, but as soon as the danger passes, the excuses begin. Often, the last boy to defend his honor and point out the cowardice of the others will be singled out for attack. Predators – even those who wear sneakers – always prey on the weak. To survive, one must be nimble.

16

Quick-witted.

A liar.

Beating their chests, such boys laugh at danger – after it has passed, of course – and boast of their fearlessness and fortitude. With disdain, they'll shake their heads in disbelief at the others, their eyes saying *How could you be afraid of such a silly thing?*

Inside their blue jeans, however, are knees that still quiver. And the blood pumping frantically through their inner ear sounds like a war drum beating for all to hear. They try to calm themselves, hoping their frightened hearts won't betray them. *Can you hear the drums?* they wonder as they eye their friends.

They're beating.

The drums are beating.

Guiding his bike over the cattle guard, Andy quickly remounted on the other side. Turning to Matt and Jeff, he said, "Thanks a lot for leaving us behind, Chickens!"

"Who you calling chicken?" Jeff snorted. "We thought you were right behind us. Didn't we Matt?"

"That's right," Matt said, trying to sound calm and unconcerned.

The drums are beating.

"You didn't even check to see if we were coming," Andy shot back. The insinuation of cowardice was clear. "You were too busy pissing your pants."

There it was.

The challenge.

"No," Matt countered with a snicker, "that was Grant."

"That's not funny!" Grant barked.

"Yeah, did you see his eyes when the light came on?" Jeff said with a grin. "He freaked."

Counterattack.

Grant was only now beginning to realize the danger he was stumbling into. Thinking quickly, he did what any self-respecting thirteen-year old would have.

He lied.

"Didn't you guys see him?"

"See who?" Matt said.

17

"The man," Grant sighed. "In the window."

"I didn't see no man."

"He was huge – and he had a shotgun."

"A shotgun!" Andy said with a smirk. "What gauge?"

"Twenty gauge – I think. It could have been a twelve."

"They both look the same, stupe!" Jeff scowled.

"Well, I don't know, it was big and it was pointed at me."

"Did you see a man with a gun?" Andy asked Matt.

"No."

"Did you?" he asked, turning to Jeff.

"No way."

"Well, I didn't see a man – or a gun. Besides, doesn't old Miss Fisher live there?"

"That's right," Jeff said triumphantly, stabbing an accusing finger at Grant. "She was my third grade teacher. I don't think it was her, though. Unless she grew. Last I saw her she was only five feet tall."

"I know what I saw," Grant persisted. "A big man with a gun and a tattoo."

"A tattoo! How did you see a tattoo?" Matt demanded. "You were in the middle of the yard! What kind of tattoo?"

"A skull!" Grant snapped back. "And it said DEATH right below it with blood dripping all goo-like from the letters."

"Bull!" Jeff snorted. "You're lying 'cause you pissed your pants and you don't want us to think you were chicken."

"I'm not the one who took off and left his friends behind," Grant reminded them.

"We already told you, we thought you were right behind us," Jeff insisted.

By this time, Andy was growing impatient with the argument. Shaking his head, he said the one thing guaranteed to stop any argument.

"Geez! You guys sound like a bunch of girls!"

To any boy biologically doped up on testosterone, the only thing worse than being called a coward was to be called a girl. Mounting their bikes, Jeff, Matt, and Grant followed Andy the

18

last half mile to Devil's Den. They rode in silence as a mist settled over the road before them. Not a thick mist, just a wispy fluff of moisture that teased the eyes.

A haze that tricked the mind.

Especially when it danced around the realistic statues of long dead soldiers. Statues that seemed to be hiding around every corner of the battlefield.

The mist made you wonder; made you wonder if that head really turned and looked at you just now? Or was it looking at you all along? Wasn't that hand at the soldier's side a moment ago? And if so, why is it reaching in your direction now?

These are the questions that run through the young minds of four boys as they patrol the darkness on two-wheeled horses of steel and plastic. On the battlegrounds of Gettysburg there is always a sensation of being watched.

The land to the right of Crawford Avenue slopped gently up from the road, blemished by jutting rocks that time and the elements had exposed.

Pock marks on the landscape.

To the left the land climbed even higher, rising from the earth like some primordial beast; a mountain troll with rocks for teeth and a hairline of rough timber at its crown.

This was Little Round Top.

To most sensible people – which excludes boys – being on the battlefield after dark would have caused a certain level of anxiety. After all, fifty thousand men were killed or wounded here in the most violent of ways. For kicks, some adventuresome souls have been known to drive through the Park after dark, their windows rolled up tight to keep out the cries of the dead and their doors locked against phantom hitchhikers. But to get on a bicycle and ride out in the open through the misty woods was another story.

The trees watched you.

The bushes listened.

This was the nighttime world of the Marauders. Over the past two years, the battlefield had suffered scores of midnight raids. Sweeping the woods and fields with their PULSAR 500 metal detector, the Marauders searched for the relics of a long ago battle. Chunks of metal they quickly sold for spending cash. They were always careful to wait until the Park closed at 10:00 before venturing out. Partly because they had to wait until their parents thought they were asleep, but mostly because using a metal detector in Gettysburg National Military Park is illegal.

To make matters worse, Matt's dad was a Park Ranger. Needless to say, to be caught on the battlefield after closing would bring the gravest of penalties. To be caught with a metal detector would be even worse.

The boys pulled into the empty parking lot in front of the massive, haphazardly thrown boulders of Devil's Den. Aptly named, this craggy formation of stone, with its natural trenches and fortifications, served well as a stronghold during the fighting at Gettysburg.

Dismounting, the Marauders pushed their wheels off the road and down to the little bridge that crossed the shallow, slow-gurgling waters of Plum Run. Without a word they laid their bikes down on the sloped ground by the creek, out of sight just in case a Ranger happened to pass by.

Taking his backpack off, Andy quickly extracted the dismantled PULSAR 500 and pieced it together. It was a task he could perform blindfolded; a skill that came in handy on those dark nights when the moon played over a faraway field.

Putting the small signal transmitter in his ear, Andy flipped the power on and tested the unit on the frame of his bike. After one minor adjustment, he was satisfied.

Looking at Matt, he said, "The woods?"

Matt nodded. "It's pretty light out right now; if it gets too dark, we can go up on the rocks."

"You coming with me?"

"Sure."

"Me and Grant'll keep a lookout for the Rangers," Jeff offered.

"Just don't yell if you see one," Andy pleaded.

"Give me some credit," Jeff snorted. "I'm not stupid."

Andy was going to say something, but thought better of it. Turning, he and Matt crossed the wooden bridge and disappeared into the murky woods beyond.

For three weeks they had worked this site, running the detector head over the ground like modern-day prospectors in search of gold. The woods around Big Round Top had thus far yielded a number of interesting and valuable artifacts, including the shell fragment Mr. Williams purchased from them that morning. The woods just across the bridge were the most fertile, especially around the public rest rooms the Park Service built years before.

There was only one problem with working the woods. In the summer, when the trees were heavy with leaves, the moon would fight a terrible battle to push its beams of precious light through the thick foliage. Often the moon lost this struggle, plunging the woods into sinister darkness – darkness meant to hide the secrets of the past.

The boys couldn't use flashlights because a Ranger would spot the light a mile away. So instead, they worked the woods by moonlight, and when the detector picked something up, they would use a special hooded flashlight to guide their digging.

On those nights when it was too dark to navigate through the trees, they worked the open ground around Devil's Den. Away from the dark woods but closer to the Hell-forged cracks and crevices of the sinister rocks.

As Andy and Matt now worked the ground under the trees with some success, Grant and Jeff listened to their muffled voices; voices heavy with the darkness and stifled by the trees.

"There's one," Andy would say and a few moments later Matt's voice would chime, "Got it." In this manner the marble pouch tied to Matt's belt began to gain weight as one bullet after another was dropped in and reunited with its kin. The deeper the boys ventured into the woods, the more like whispers their voices became, blending with the night sounds.

Sitting under a tree next to the bridge, Jeff leaned his head back against the cool trunk, closed his eyes, and let his mind wander. *Some poor Reb could have died right where I'm sitting,* he thought. Quickly, he opened his eyes and forced the image from his mind.

Never speak of the dead.

Don't even think of them.

That was the unwritten code the Marauders adhered to with religious reverence. They never talked about the men who died on these rocks.

In these woods.

On these fields.

Not while they were out here.

And most certainly not in the dark.

If they were compelled to talk about the battle, they would do so when safely behind the protective walls of Fort Apache. When they were on the battlefield, they tried not to think about the relics they were collecting. Tried keeping their minds from pondering the origin of the lead bullets they dug from the earth. Wondering whose arm or leg or chest or head that bullet passed through before being trampled into the mud and lost for a hundred and thirty-one years.

They tried not to think of these things, but the images played in their minds anyway; nightmares that walked a thin line between the conscious and subconscious.

An hour passed before Andy and Matt emerged from the woods with the marble sack bursting at Matt's waist. In Matt's hand was a prize none of them had expected: a Confederate belt buckle. At first glance it appeared to be in rough condition but experience had taught them that a good cleaning would improve the buckle's condition considerably. The elements had been kind to it. They were fortunate.

Tearing down the PULSAR 500, Andy stuffed it back in his knapsack and hoisted it onto his back.

"Look what I've got," Matt said as he reached into his own pack and extracted a silver labeled can of Busch Light.

"Beer!" Jeff said with flaring nostrils. "Where'd you get it?"

"My dad has a whole case in the fridge. It's been there a couple weeks so he probably doesn't even remember how many are left."

"What if he does?" Andy asked.

Matt shrugged. "He can't prove I took it. I'll just play dumb."

"That won't be hard," Jeff chortled.

Raising his clenched fist, Matt let the knuckles hover a few inches from Jeff's nose.

His point was grasped with perfect clarity.

"I was just kidding," Jeff pouted, putting his open hands up to shield his face from the impending attack. "Geez, no one can take a joke anymore."

Lowering his fist, Matt said, "I can take you, and you're a joke."

"Ha, ha."

"Who wants a drink?" Matt asked, hoisting the beer aloft.

"Me," Grant piped in immediately.

"Me too," Jeff said.

"I'll drink some," Andy said, "but let's go somewhere else. This place gives me the creeps."

"The Wheatfield?" Matt offered.

"Okay."

Mounting their bikes, the boys backtracked along Crawford Avenue to Wheatfield Road. A shorter route would have been to follow Crawford until it connected with Ayres Avenue, but this would have entailed a drive through the woods. Not something the boys were eager to do unless absolutely necessary. When you're riding a bike quickly – like boys do when traveling through a spooky forest at midnight – the wind whistles loudly in your ears, making it hard to hear. And since every boy learns at an early age, usually around six or seven, that monsters, ghouls, and ghosts only attack when you can't hear them coming, the path through the woods was strictly taboo.

Pulling off the road onto a well-worn footpath, the Marauders raced their bikes to the center of the notorious Wheatfield. During the second day of fighting at Gettysburg, four thousand dead and wounded piled up on this small parcel of land. Four thousand men wearing blue and gray. Four thousand men stained red by the brutality of war. A century later, all that remained was an empty field and a few scattered trees.

Dropping their bikes under an oak, Matt pulled the beer from his pack and popped the top as the others flopped to the ground. Putting the cool aluminum to his lips, he filled his cheeks with the brew – then spewed half of it out as he tried to swallow. "Good stuff," he croaked, quickly handing the can to Andy.

Dutifully, Andy took a sip and handed the can to Jeff, and in his turn Jeff handed it to Grant. After another pass, the beer was empty. Crushing the can in his hand, actually, in both hands, Jeff belched. "Good brewski," he said, trying to hold down the bile that was rising in his throat.

The others were quick to voice their appreciation of the hops and barley with nods and smiles all around.

Hypocrites one and all.

Lying on their backs in the middle of the Wheatfield, their heads resting softly in cradling hands, the boys stared off into the night sky. There is something about lying on one's back in the middle of a field that makes you appreciate the magnitude of the universe, the eternity of space. Though they all felt the awe, it was Andy who put their feelings to words.

"It's weird, don't you think? The entire world is behind us right now and all we have to do is step out into space. This must be what eternity feels like."

At one o'clock they headed back to town.

4

Sunday, May 15
9:20 a.m.

Wheeler's Quick-E Mart was on the corner of Route 15 and Baltimore Pike, prime real estate that would make any developer drool. It was at the hub of all the tourist traffic. Near the shops, near the tour bus office, near National Cemetery. Art and June Wheeler knew what they had in their little store and they weren't about to give it up.

The year before, after forty years in business and many offers to buy them out, the mom and pop store upgraded its image in an attempt to compete with the franchises springing up all over town.

The upgrades included a name change from Wheeler's to the Quick-E Mart; though everyone in town still called it Wheeler's. There were two new rows of gas pumps with automated credit card readers, and the sagging face of the store got a much needed lift and tuck.

It now sported a classic diner car look.

And, of course, the freezers and refrigerators that served the Wheelers reliably for four decades were quietly retired to the fate of all unwanted relics. They were now permanent residents of the county landfill.

R.I.P.

Lime green squirt guns were a buck fifty at Wheeler's. Mass produced at a factory in Somewhereville, Illinois, the little guns were crude replicas of the German Luger. Though it's doubtful the Germans would have approved of the color.

A buck fifty.

Andy thought the price a little steep, but on a Sunday morning in Gettysburg, Wheeler's was the only place nearby that was open. Fishing five quarters, two dimes and a nickel out of his pocket, then having to dig for another eight cents in tax, Andy grudgingly handed the money over to June Wheeler.

He needed a squirt gun – even if it was *lime* green.

On the sidewalk in front of the Quick-E Mart, Andy unzipped his backpack and extracted a half-liter soda bottle filled with a shampoo and water solution. Pulling the stopper from the back of the squirt gun, he carefully filled the pistol with the liquid. Topping the gun off, he spilled a few drops on his hand. Wiping the spillage off on his jeans, he quickly pressed the stopper back in place and then capped the bottle.

Andy was afraid of dogs; had been since the age of five when his aunt's dachshund, Chester, bit him on the calf. He still had the scar. Two little pockmarks where the long-eared, Doberman wanna-be clamped onto him.

Now, seven years later, Andy was faced with a new threat. A mongrel that went by the name of Duke. No small dog, Duke was one of those mutts you could saddle up and pass off as a really ugly pony. He belonged to the Cole family at the corner of Breckenridge Street and Long Lane and was frequently allowed to roam free in the community park near his house. Barbara Cole saw the wretched dog at the pound the week before and somehow fell in love with the cur.

Duke wasn't necessarily a bad dog, he was just a big dog. A big dog that liked to chase bikes. The harder the bike tried to get away from him, the more Duke enjoyed it. He still had a bruised lip from a rear tire he managed to catch two days before. Of course, once he caught it he didn't quite know what to do with it. But that didn't matter. The thrill was in the chase; and Duke loved the chase.

Holding the gun close to his chest so that it was pointing straight up, Andy sneered out of the corner of his mouth, "Bond. James Bond. Let me introduce you to chemical warfare, Herr Duke." Aiming at the filthy brown garbage can at the corner of the walk, he pulled the trigger.

Bull's-eye.

Blowing nonexistent smoke from the barrel, Andy slid the gun into a makeshift holster strapped to the frame of his bike. Turning onto West Street, he started for Jeff's house.

Okay, Duke, he thought as he rode, *I've got a little surprise for you. Mess with the best, die like the rest.*

But Duke was nowhere to be seen this Sunday morning.

No bark.

No growl.

No chase.

No Duke.

This didn't bother Andy in the least; he was glad for it. Although he did wonder where the dog had gotten off to. *Was there a sudden demand for pony rides*? he mused, smiling at his own humor.

It didn't matter. Duke's absence was the important thing. Andy took comfort in knowing that chemical weapons have a long shelf life.

5

Fort Apache was nestled halfway up a hundred-year old oak tree on the back property line of the Kowalski homestead. It was a monstrous bird nest of unwanted plywood, planks, rope and ten-penny nails. Like all *true* tree forts, it was painted in camouflage green and brown. To improve Fort Apache's overall external appearance, the boys painted a red and white bull's-eye on the side.

A tattered and stained Jolly Roger – the pirates' infamous skull and crossbones – flew from a makeshift mast at the top of the fort. Jeff discovered this treasure at a yard sale the previous summer. It now served dutifully as the fort's crowning touch; a monument to swashbucklers past and present.

Fort Apache was every boy's dream.

Inside, the Marauders had taken modern art to a new extreme. Their "couch" once served time doing hard labor as the bench seat in a 1956 Chevy pickup. During the mid-sixties someone got the silly notion that an imitation sheepskin would look nice draped over the seat.

It didn't.

Thirty years later the sheepskin was still there, but no one would have recognized it as such. And though any God-fearing person would have cringed at the sight of the hideous couch, the Marauders considered it a prize possession. It took three pulleys, a hundred feet of rope, and four sweating, grunting Marauders to hoist the seat aloft. Now that it was safely inside Fort Apache, it was a good bet that the tree would have to fall over before the couch ever saw solid ground again.

Opposite the couch slumped a bean bag chair that Grant's father purchased in the early seventies; a fact heinously evident by its color.

Neon green.

Sometimes at night, when boredom stalked Fort Apache, the Marauders would shine their heavy duty flashlight at the chair for a minute, then click the high-power beam off and plunge the fort into darkness. Debate still raged as to whether or not the chair actually glowed after doing this, but Grant and Jeff were convinced of it.

The chair's original stuffing had seeped out of its vinyl casing some years before. In its place, the boys stuffed crumpled newspapers, old T-shirts, even a pair of dirty socks that Jeff had thrown in for good luck.

Adorning the north wall was one of Jeff's former pets, a praying mantis called Legs. Jeff had the pet only two days before accidentally leaving Legs' cage – a Mason jar – out in the sun too long. A severe case of heatstroke finished Legs off in short order.

A pin now kept him attached firmly to the wall.

As for the rest of the interior, it was carefully papered with pictures of Geena Davis, Jeff's one true love. Most of the pictures came from sleazy tabloids, but there were several full-length posters Jeff managed to glean from yard sales and movie theaters. A picture pecking order was established early in the wallpapering process. Basically, the more revealing the outfit Geena was wearing, the more prominently the photo was displayed.

Although Andy, Matt, and Grant enjoyed the three hundred and sixty degree view, they often argued that a few commando, football, or race car photos were in order. Jeff ignored these entreaties whenever they were raised and since it was his fort, there was little the others could do.

Geena stayed.

* * *

Sitting on the couch with the others crowding around him, Andy leafed through a sportsman's magazine, eyes scanning each page quickly before turning to the next.

"Shoot! I had the page marked," Andy muttered. "Now I can't find it." Halfway through the catalogue his eyes locked onto the advertisement.

"Here it is."

"Read it," Matt said.

"All right," Andy said, scanning the page. "It says, 'For the discriminating treasure hunter, the PULSAR 7000 offers the latest in detection technology. With its' twelve-inch depth capability, even the most elusive treasures will be within your reach.' And then it gives the price. Two hundred and thirty-nine dollars."

Turning to Jeff, Grant asked, "Are we discriminating?"

Producing his best stiff-upper-lip, Jeff huffed, "But of course, Lord Wilson." Turning to Matt, he crooned, "Pardon me, but do you have any Grey Poupon?"

Matt rolled his eyes and ignored the pair. "How deep does ours go?" he asked Andy.

"Only four or five inches."

"You think we could find more stuff if we had the 7000?"

"Uh-huh. Maybe not bullets," Andy said, "because they'd be near the surface anyway. But I bet there's a lot of shells embedded in the ground out there. They probably buried themselves when they hit, that's why we don't find many fragments. Better yet, if someone's already gone over an area, the PULSAR 7000 will pick up stuff they missed. I think we should do it."

29

"Where we gonna get the money?" Grant asked. "Two hundred and some dollars–"

"Two hundred thirty-nine," Andy said.

"Two hundred thirty-nine dollars is a lot of money."

"How much do we have in the treasury?" Jeff asked.

Matt pulled a crumpled paper from his shirt pocket. "Twelve dollars, forty-five cents."

"That means we need . . ."

"Two hundred and twenty-seven dollars," Andy said, strumming his fingers across his knee.

Jeff whistled. "That's a lot."

"Listen!" Andy insisted, growing impatient at his friends' lack of vision. "We can do this. If we put half our earnings into the treasury every week, we'll have the money by the end of summer."

"It's still a lot of money," Grant said.

Throwing his hands up in the air, Andy started to show his exasperation. "We'll make three times what we're making now once we have the new detector."

"Andy's right," Matt stated firmly. "If this thing can go down twelve inches, there's no telling what we'll find. We only get forty or fifty cents for a bullet, depending on how many Mr. Williams can sell. With this new detector we might find more buckles and shells and stuff like that. We could make a killing."

Jeff shrugged. "Sounds good to me, I guess."

"All right," Grant sighed. "I guess it's the smart thing to do."

Andy grinned. "Great! From now on we'll give half our money to Matt for the treasury. The other half we'll split four ways like always. Agreed?"

"Agreed," the others sang in chorus.

"Shake," Andy said, putting his hand out, palm down.

The others stood and placed their hands over Andy's, then they shook. With that, the deal was as firm as a Wall Street contract.

Agreements are so much simpler when you're young.

6

Burke Holtz was an unsavory character by any rational standard. He was a two-hundred pound eighth-grader who wore the same clothes day after day. What made matters worse was that Burke viewed bathing as optional; and washing his clothes usually amounted to shaking them twice in the wind. His classmates once tallied forty-seven straight days that Burke wore the same green corduroy pants and striped blue shirt.

Burke was disliked by his classmates. Not because of his disgusting hygiene or compulsive eating – kids can sometimes be quite forgiving in those areas. No. It was because, like the rest of the Holtz clan, Burke was a nasty cuss.

Nasty with a capital N.

At the age of fourteen, he had already been arrested twice for shoplifting. While most would be ashamed of such a stigma, Burke was proud of his record, strutting it around like it was a badge of honor pinned to his chest.

He was a bully.

Bully with a capital B.

Like all bullies, Burke enjoyed picking on boys smaller than himself. Boys too weak or timid to fight back. His father proudly displayed a 'My kid beat up your Honor Roll Student' bumper sticker in the rear window of his dilapidated 1973 Ford pickup.

Now, someone once said that the acorn doesn't fall far from the tree, and in Burke's case they weren't far from the truth. In twenty years he'd probably tip the scale at over three hundred pounds, just like his father. He'd probably drive the same run-down old pickup, too; beer cans rattling around in the rusty bed every time the truck turned a corner. With luck he wouldn't spawn any offspring, sparing the world further insult.

Dropping a pair of quarters into the soda machine in the hallway on the first floor, next to the gym, Andy pushed the Diet Coke button and listened to the clunk of the machine as it dropped the can into the dispenser. Reaching down for the soda, he was slammed violently into the machine from behind.

"Hey, Martin," a familiar voice hissed in his ear. The words carried the stench of rancid breath exhaled over teeth that hadn't seen a toothbrush in weeks.

Turning around, Andy looked with contempt into Burke's eyes. Before he could move, Burke's forearm slammed into Andy's throat, pinning him to the soda machine. With his free hand the bully reached down and plucked the Diet Coke from the dispenser. Running his nasty tongue around the top of the can and down the side, Burke held it out to Andy.

"Want it back?" he purred, dancing the can in front of Andy's nose. Andy didn't reply, he just stared at the bully with loathing eyes. Grinning, Burke spat on the wall next to Andy's head, then relaxed his strangle hold as he popped open the Coke. Gulping down half the soda – seemingly in one swallow – he leaned forward and belched loudly in Andy's face.

"Got a problem with that, Martin?" he leered.

They were familiar words to Andy; familiar and annoying.

"I said," Burke snarled, jabbing a fat finger in Andy's chest, "Got a problem with that?"

"No!" Andy snapped.

"Watch it," the bully cautioned, waving his finger in Andy's face. "Your boyfriend ain't around to protect you."

Andy clenched his fists, but remained silent.

Tossing the half-finished Coke at Andy and spilling some on his shirt, Burke turned and strutted away.

Matt was just coming out of the gym as Burke rumbled around the corner at the end of the hall. One look at Andy told Matt all he needed to know.

"Again?"

Andy shrugged, "He's a half-wit. What do you expect?"

"I'll kill him," Matt hissed. Throwing his gym bag to the floor, he started after the long-gone Burke Holtz.

Andy grabbed him by the arm as he passed.

"Let it go, Matt. I'll get him in my own time, in my own way." With a twinkle in his eye, he said, "I've got plans for Burke. Big plans."

7

Devil's Den
Friday, May 20

There's one," Andy said, holding the detector's disc perfectly still an inch above the ground. The hum in his ear was steady and clear, a good sign. Crouching, Matt stuck his gardening spade into the hard earth and extracted a four-inch core. Dumping the dirt on the ground, he sifted through it.

"Rock . . . rock . . . rock," Matt called out as he systematically weeded through the soil. "This might be it," he said, pausing to pick up a crusted chunk of metal that looked too flat to be a bullet. Brushing it on his pants, he held it up to the dim light.

His face soured. "It's only a nickel."

"What year?"

Rubbing the face of the coin, Matt turned it back and forth in the light, trying to read the numbers in the lower right corner.

"Nineteen sixty-nine," he said. "It might be sixty-seven. Hard to tell."

Curling the corner of his mouth down, Andy said, "It's not worth a thing."

"It's worth a nickel," Matt said, dropping the coin in his pouch. Looking up at Andy, he said, "Every coin can't be old and valuable. Just like every bullet can't be in perfect condition."

33

"I know, I know. I just want that PULSAR 7000 and so far we're not doing so well."

"We're doing fine. We've been here an hour and we have thirteen bullets – and forty-seven cents."

Andy smiled. "Right. Sorry. Guess I'm impatient."

"Surprise, surprise," Matt said with a grin.

Before Andy could say anything, footsteps raced up the path, sounding terribly loud in the quiet forest.

Slap-slap-slap!

Wump-wump-wump!

"Headlights!" Jeff shouted as he and Grant rounded a corner, panting heavily for breath.

"Are the bikes out of sight?" Matt asked, his eyes darting up the path.

"Next to the creek where we left them," Grant answered.

"It's probably a Ranger," Jeff wheezed.

"Has to be," Andy said. "The Park's been closed for two hours. They're probably just doing a drive-by. Let's go back where we can see."

Crouching in the trees a few yards from the bridge, the boys watched the headlights approach slowly along Crawford Avenue. By now they could tell it was a Bronco. Crossing the cattle guard by Warren Avenue, the Bronco continued it's approach. Pulling off to the shoulder, it stopped in the parking area directly in front of the bridge.

A spotlight came on.

"Stay down," Andy hissed as the boys tried to melt into the cold ground.

Shining the light on the rest rooms across the bridge, the Ranger seemed satisfied that they were secure. Flipping off the light and picking up a clipboard from the passenger seat, he made a note. Setting the clipboard back down, he paused long enough to change radio stations, then put the Bronco in gear and continued his slow drive up and around Devil's Den.

The boys waited until they could no longer hear the engine before emerging from the trees.

"That was your dad," Andy said to Matt.

34

"Maybe we should call it a night," Jeff offered.

"Not yet," Matt said. "He'll see us going up Wheatfield Road. Let's wait a few minutes. Give him time to get back to the station."

Pulling their bikes from the incline next to the creek, they walked to the parking lot and waited. Realizing that he was still holding the metal detector, Andy squatted down and disassembled the unit, stuffing it in his knapsack.

"What the heck?" Jeff snapped. Elbowing Grant, he said, "Look! Over there!"

Glancing up in time to see Jeff point toward Devil's Den, Andy peered across the road with the others. "What in the world?" he muttered to himself. "How long has *he* been there?"

Across the road, sitting quietly on the rocks, was a boy who looked to be about fourteen or fifteen. The Marauders knew every boy in town and this one was definitely not a local. Andy quickly assumed that he was a re-enactor, mostly because he was dressed in a Union outfit that was dirty and disheveled. In several places the material was torn and he could see that two buttons were missing from the well-worn frock coat.

Resting his chin on one knee, the boy stared vacantly off into empty space. He appeared to take no notice of the Marauders who were only a few dozen yards away. Instead, the boy seemed to be contemplating something; something rather serious.

"Look at that," Grant said. "He's pretending like he doesn't see us. Bet he's been spying on us the whole time."

"What do we do?" Jeff asked, fidgeting nervously. "What if he talks to the Rangers?"

"Why would he do that?" Matt scoffed. "Besides, if he was going to talk to the Rangers, he would have stopped my dad and told him already."

"Well, what do we do then? Go talk to him?"

"Why not," Andy said, and before they could stop him he started across the street toward the midnight intruder. Matt, Jeff and Grant scrambled to catch up, not wanting to be the last to follow Andy's lead – lest they be called cowards.

"What're you doing?" Andy asked when he was only two dozen feet from the boy. "Are you lost?"

Looking up with a start, the boy jumped to his feet.

"I've lost m'drum," he stammered.

Then, as they looked on, the strange fellow vanished before their very eyes. Turning into a mist that melted into the night.

It only took a moment for reality to sink in.

About as long as it takes to yell *Ghost*!

Shrieking as if Hell's hounds were loose and hot on their heels, the boys scrambled for their bikes and raced out of the Park faster than they had ever ridden in their lives.

As they fled in terror, a pair of ghostly eyes watched them from atop Devil's Den.

Curious eyes.

If the boys had stopped for a moment and listened they would have heard a voice echo down from the rocks.

A sad voice.

"I've lost m'drum," it said.

But no one heard.

8

Saturday, May 21

The music box sat in the center of the bed; sat there silently, yet eager to sing. It was a delicate music box, with two white ceramic rabbits frolicking around a seated lamb. It seemed oddly out of place resting on a bedspread covered with football players.

Picking the box up, Matt quickly wound it, then set it gently back on the bed and listened to it play. Inside, a little metal instrument that was the soul of the music box began to turn and the cheerful tune *"It's A Small World After All"* began to play. As it played, tears gathered in Matt's eyes. He fought the tears, as he always did, but lost the battle, as he always had.

The music box once belonged to Matt's mother, a birthday gift Matt's father gave to her just before they were married. It was all Matt had left to remember her by, that and a few photographs.

They were living ten miles outside Butte, Montana, when she died of breast cancer in August 1986. Matt was only five when she died, but he remembered her.

He remembered her smile and the way she laughed, always covering her mouth with those delicate fingers of hers. Her face was just an image now, a memory of beauty and grace embedded in Matt's mind. A smiling image wrapped in the fading echo of sweet laughter.

"Take care of this for me, darling," she whispered as she handed Matt the box in weak, trembling hands. "If you ever miss me, remember that I love you very much." Then, her strength almost spent, she pulled Matt close and kissed him on the cheek.

An hour later she died.

After Ann Jacobs' death, Matt's father applied for a Ranger position in Gettysburg and they moved east. Still grieving over the loss of his wife, Steve Jacobs was running away from the house and the yard and the street that held so many powerful, painful memories. He gave most of his wife's things to Ann's sister, but Matt wouldn't let him take the music box. It was his now; a symbol of his mother's love.

Letting the music play out, Matt placed the ceramic box back in its original container and cushioned it with the same old, yellowed tissue he had first wrapped it in years before.

He wondered about the ghost at Devil's Den. Wondered if there really was a Heaven. Wondered if the soul kept on living after the body died.

His mother believed that; believed in God and eternal life and all those things that seem so impossible and at the same time so undeniable. She told him she was going to Heaven and he hoped this was true because then he would see her again. That was what Matt Jacobs wanted more than anything; to see his mother again.

To hug her and never let her go. To feel her sweet kiss on his cheek.

One kiss, from a mother to her son.

That was all he wanted.

It was a simple little wish that he made every year when he blew out the candles on his birthday cake. It was a dream he kept alive in his heart with every Christmas angel he saw; angels that reminded him of where his mother might be – where she *had* to be.

Kneeling next to the bed, Matt slid the music box back into its hiding place.

"I can't stop thinking about you, Mom," he whispered. "I wish you were here." Wiping the tears from his eyes, he picked up his backpack and slung it over his shoulders. Walking to the mirror behind his bedroom door, he stared at his reflection, waiting for his red eyes to fade.

He couldn't let the others see his tears.

Andy, yes. He would understand.

But not Jeff or Grant.

Matt Jacobs was the Titan; the strength of the Marauders. Never to cry, never to show fear, never to back down. Matt was always the one they turned to when their courage needed bolstering. Taking a deep breath, he put his mask – his Titan's mask – back on his little-boy face.

They were waiting for him at Fort Apache.

Titans never cry.

9

Saturday, May 21

"It *was* a ghost," Andy said in disgust. "Not a funny mist, or a mass hallucination." He threw Grant a look of disappointment.

"I don't believe in ghosts!" Jeff said firmly, shaking his head and waving his hands in front of him. "I don't! I don't! I don't!"

"What did you see then, pea-brain? What was it? I saw it, Grant saw it, Matt saw it, and you, even you saw it." Throwing his hands in the air, Andy fumed, "I don't understand why you all want to pretend we didn't see it. It was a GHOST! You all can stick your heads in the sand if you want. I know what I saw and I'm not afraid to admit it."

"I already told you I believe–" Matt started to protest, but Andy waved him off.

"I know. I didn't mean you. I meant Wuss number one and Wuss number two. Afraid of a ghost. I know plenty of girls who wouldn't be afraid of a ghost if they saw one."

Ah, at last, the challenge.

"I'm not afraid of no ghost!" Jeff shot back.

"Me neither," Grant said. "I was just trying to think of a logical explanation."

Challenge met.

"Why do you have to try and explain it, Mr. Professor?" Andy said. "Why can't you just accept what you saw? A lot of people died around here – and most of them died in a bad way. Maybe a few of them are still around."

Tossing a dog-eared book on the sofa, Andy said, "I've been doing some reading. My dad got this book last year and I never thought much of it until last night, after I got home."

Picking the book up, Jeff read the title. "Gettysburg Ghosts." With a pensive look on his face, a face that wasn't often frequented by pensive looks, he said, "Yeah, I remember seeing this book. What of it?"

"Well," Andy said, "if you had read it you'd know there are lots of ghosts around here. In houses that were around during the Civil War, on the battlefield, all over the place."

"Places like Devil's Den?" Matt asked.

"Exactly."

"Just 'cause someone writes a book about it doesn't mean it's true," Grant argued. "Didn't you ever see those magazine covers about the president being abducted by aliens? It's the same thing."

"No it isn't!" Andy shot back. "The guy who wrote this book used to be a Ranger here. If anyone's gonna know about ghosts around here, it's gonna be a Ranger."

"Why don't we ask Matt's dad then?" Jeff offered.

"Brilliant," Andy quipped. "And when he asks us what we were doing at Devil's Den in the middle of the night, what should we tell him?"

"We don't have to tell him that part," Jeff replied with a scowl. "Why can't we just ask him about ghosts in general, you know, like we're curious or something?"

Matt shook his head. "He'd figure something's up. He's pretty quick about things like that. I say we go ask Mr. Williams. Maybe he's heard about a ghost around Devil's Den. Besides, if he figures out that we've been on the battlefield at night, I don't think he'll rat us out to our parents."

"Yeah," Jeff nodded. "Mr. Williams is cool."

"Good then, it's settled," Matt said. "We'll go to the Emporium and see if he's got time to talk to us."

Standing, Jeff was the first down the side of the old oak, using boards that were nailed to the tree as foot and hand holds. Grant followed closely behind, clinging to each board as if it were a life ring and he was being tossed in heavy seas. This was the only thing about being a Marauder that Grant hated; navigating Fort Apache's rickety ladder. At one point he even went as far as to suggest moving the fort to the base of the tree. But the others scoffed at this idea. Tree forts were meant to be *in* trees, not under them.

It was that simple.

Stepping out onto the makeshift ladder, Matt stopped and stared at Andy who was sitting on the couch with furrows of deep concentration marking his forehead.

Contemporary artists would have been inspired by the image. The wrinkled brow of a young man pondering the mysteries of life and death. Too young for such concerns, but concerned nonetheless.

"What's wrong?" Matt asked, studying Andy's face.

40

"Just thinking."

"About?"

Andy looked up. "I was thinking about what the ghost said when we walked up."

"What about it?"

"He said 'I've lost my drum.' " Andy shrugged. "I was just wondering why he would say that to us."

Shaking his head, Matt said, "You think too much, Martin. Come on, let's go."

Then he disappeared down the side of the tree.

But the question remained.

I've lost m'drum.

10

The Civil War Emporium
12:30 P.M.

Ed was behind the counter showing a Confederate belt buckle replica to an academic-looking customer when the boys entered the Emporium. Looking up for a moment, he shot the boys a smile, then continued his sales pitch. With an I'll-think-about-it nod, which really meant thanks-but-no-thanks, the customer drifted off toward the book racks and the T-shirts. With a shrug, Ed placed the buckle back in the display case under the counter and locked the sliding panel.

"What you boys up to?" Ed asked, leaning over the counter with a big grin. "Thought you'd be in this morning. Clair – you remember Clair, don't you? She owns the place next door." Winking, he said, "I think she's got her eye on me. Anyway, she dropped off some homemade cinnamon buns right after I opened and I saved some for you boys."

41

"All right!" Jeff said, patting his stomach.

"They sat here all morning," Ed continued. "Well, most of the morning. They kind of disappeared, one by one. That Clair, she makes a mean cinnamon bun."

The glimmer in Jeff's eyes died as he realized the cinnamon buns were gone. Holding his stomach, he could feel it churn and hear it grumble as all hope of a pastry heaven perished.

Looking at the boys with curious eyes, then glancing down at their empty hands, Ed said, "No bullets? Every Saturday you boys come in here to sell your bullets. What gives? I been paying you too much?" He laughed. "You getting lazy on me?"

"I knew we forgot something," Grant muttered.

"We got something important to ask you about, Mr. Williams, but you gotta promise not to tell anyone," Andy said.

Ed crossed his heart, saying, "Stick a needle in my eye."

The boys looked at each other for a moment, not quite sure how to approach the subject. In the end, all eyes turned to Andy. By silent vote, he was elected spokesman.

Looking Ed right in the eye, Andy came directly to the point. "Do you believe in ghosts?"

"Ghosts, huh?" Mr. Williams mused, sitting slowly in his chair. He pushed himself back until he was balanced on the two hind legs with his back against the wall.

"Well, yeah. S'pose I do believe in ghosts. You get to my age and you start believing in all sorts of things. Hell, boys, I'm sixty years old. At best I've got ten, twenty, maybe thirty years left in me – and that's if I'm lucky. Much as I like my bacon and eggs, it's more likely ten years than thirty. When you get that close to the Reaper, you start believing in a whole lot of things. Believe you me. You have to."

"Do you think you become a ghost when you die?" Andy pressed.

"Sure I do. Well, not exactly a ghost. I believe the spirit is released from the body."

"But how do you know?"

"I don't"

Andy gave him a quizzical look.

"Look," Ed said. "Do you believe in God?"

Andy nodded.

"How 'bout Heaven?"

"Yeah."

"Then you got to believe that there's a spirit buried someplace in that puny little thing you call a body, right?" He poked a meaty finger into Andy's shoulder for emphasis. "And when the body dies, it only makes sense that the spirit would leave."

"How come we can't see the spirits of all the people that have died, then?" Jeff challenged. "I mean, there's millions of dead people, right?"

"Billions."

"Then how come we can't see them?"

Ed leaned forward, letting the chair flop down on all fours. With a wrinkled brow and a pensive stare, he said, "Most go to Heaven, or to Hell, but I guess some of them get lost now and then."

The boys exchanged silent looks.

Glancing around the semicircle of young faces, Ed nodded slowly and quietly asked the next logical question. "You boys seen a ghost?" His eyes told them he already knew the truth.

"Last night," Andy said. "At Devil's Den."

"What the blazes you boys doing out there after dark?" Ed growled. "You know the Park closes at ten." Raising his hands in surrender, he quickly said, "Never mind, I don't want to know. Just tell me what you saw."

"It was a kid, just like us," Jeff piped in, "only maybe a couple years older."

"That's right," Matt said, "and he was wearin' a Federal uniform."

"He said he lost his drum, so we figured he was a drummer from one of the Union regiments that fought around Devil's Den," Andy offered. "That was the Fifth Corps, right?"

"Among others. If I remember right, Third Corps and Second Corps were out there, too. But you're probably right, the Fifth

Corps saw a lot of action around the Den. Your ghost could have been with one of the four regiments in Colonel Vincent's brigade. They held the Union flank on the second day of the battle, but I bet you knew that, didn't you?" Though all the boys nodded, it was Andy the old proprietor was looking at.

"Colonel Chamberlain's 20th Maine," Andy said softly, his mind wandering over the possibilities. "You think our ghost might have been a drummer for Colonel Chamberlain?"

"Might have."

"But wasn't the Third Brigade – Vincent's Brigade – up on Little Round Top?"

"Yeah, now that you mention it, I think you're right. Guess I got a soft spot for the old 20th Maine. Wishful thinking. But then, who knows?" Raising a less-than-cynical eyebrow, he added, "It is possible. Let's see, aside from Chamberlain's 20th Maine, there was the 83rd Pennsylvania, the 44th New York and, let's see . . . damn! There was a fourth regiment under Vincent. What was that fourth regiment?"

"The 16th Michigan, wasn't it?" Andy said.

"That's it. I always forget the 16th Michigan."

"You think the ghost died at Devil's Den?" Grant asked. Only afterwards did he stop to think how strange it was to ask such a question.

"Well," Ed sighed, "assuming it was a ghost you saw and not just a figment of your imagination–" stopping abruptly, Ed's eyes narrowed, "You boys haven't been eating any wild mushrooms or anything like that, have you?" He peered intently into their eyes – as if by doing so he could tell if they were lying. When they all shook their heads in adamant denial, Ed nodded, "Good. Well, like I was saying, if it really was a ghost, I guess he probably did die around Devil's Den. Or up on Little Round Top," he added, still rooting for the 20th Maine.

"Why do you think he's spooking around Devil's Den?" Jeff asked. "Is he lost?"

"Well, boys, some people say that when a person dies suddenly, violently, the spirit doesn't realize it's dead and just hangs around, watching other people live their lives." Looking at the boys, he added, "That's what they say, anyway. I got a friend who lives just outside of town in a house that was used as a field hospital during the battle. He tells me that sometimes when he and his wife wake up in the morning they can smell bread baking throughout the house. Only thing is there's no bread. Sometimes they see someone walk from one room to another, but when they go to see who it is there's no one there. It's kind of eerie if you think about it."

"Cool," the boys sang in chorus.

Ed chuckled at their enthusiasm. "I bet you wouldn't think it was so cool if you heard footsteps in your attic," he said. "Or the rattle of a door knob that shouldn't be turning. I'll tell you one thing: after living in that house all these years, I know my friends believe in ghosts."

The boys were silent, drinking it in, mouths open in awe.

"Yep," Ed said. "You boys are probably living in the most haunted town in America."

"You've lived here a long time," Matt said after a moment. "Did you ever see anything funny?"

Ed didn't answer right away, he just stared at the boys, his fingers strumming the glass-topped counter.

"Well?" Andy pressed.

Ed nodded. "I've seen a few strange things."

"Like what?"

Looking around to make sure none of his customers were within earshot, Ed Williams leaned close to the boys and uttered one word: "Campfires."

"Campfires?" Andy said.

Ed nodded. "Bonfires, actually. Up on Cemetery Ridge. I was driving home one night, oh, I guess around one o'clock, and I saw a flickering light up on the hill. Then there was another, and another, until there must have been thirty or forty of them. I didn't know what the hell was going on so I called the Rangers and told them what I saw. Next morning they came around the store and told me what they found."

"What'd they find?" Grant asked eagerly.

"Nothing. Not a damn thing. No fires. No embers. Nothing. I told those Rangers that I was sure of what I saw."

Stopping, he eyed the boys.

"Wanna know what they said?"

"What?"

"They said they believed me. Said they got calls about once every three or four months reporting strange fires. Well, I tell you, at that point I didn't know if I believed in ghosts or not, but I know that Pennsylvania don't grow fireflies that big."

"Way cool!" Grant said.

"I thought you didn't believe in ghosts!" Matt said, punching Grant in the arm.

Ed chuckled.

"I never said that," Grant protested, massaging his injured biceps.

"Did you ever see the fires again?" Andy asked.

"Only one other time," Ed replied. "Right after a Confederate soldier ran into the path of my headlights and vanished before my eyes. I slammed on my brakes and jumped out of the car, wondering where in the hell he got off to, and there, not a hundred feet from the road, were all these campfires. Dozens of 'em. I could see men gathered around them, but nothing clear, just shadows. Real strange. After a minute they started to, well, sort of wink out, I guess, and then it got really dark and I got the hell out of there."

Ed shook his head and snorted what was almost a laugh. "It's funny. We spend our lives stumbling down the road of hedonistic pleasures, looking for meaning and purpose in all the chaos life spits out, but looking in the wrong places. Always in the wrong places. When we get near the end of the road, we suddenly embrace God and religion. You know why?"

The boys shook their heads.

"Because we're afraid of what lies beyond the grave."

"What's hedonistic?" Grant asked.

"Hedonistic? Well, a hedonist is someone who believes life is about pleasure, the pursuit of pleasure, and everything they do centers on attaining pleasure. Hell, I've had my share of pleasure.

46

Plenty of pain, too. But once your sun starts setting over that horizon, before that final ray of sunlight is snuffed out for good, you start reconsidering things. At least most people do."

"Uh-huh," Grant nodded, as if he understood.

"You begin to wonder if things just all of a sudden stop and you cease to exist. You know, a big blackness. That's what atheists believe. But I'd hate to think that's the way it ends. Hell, I don't know. I always believed in God in my heart, I guess. Haven't necessarily lived like I believe in Him, but now that my sun is setting, I guess I got to start acting a little more Christian, huh?"

Looking at each of the boys in turn, Mr. Williams said, "What a bunch of hypocrites we are. The whole lot of us."

His voice was rising now.

"A bunch of hypocrites. It's just like at Easter. Suddenly the church is packed like Wal-Mart on Christmas Eve as the faithful pile in. Faithful!" he snorted. "Hypocrites are what they are!"

A customer was hovering near the end of the counter now, a poster of Pickett's Charge clutched tightly in her hands. She looked like a nervous rabbit; not sure whether she should put the poster on the counter or just drop it back in its bin and slip quietly out the door.

Glancing at her, then back at the boys, Ed said, "I got customers, boys." With a wink, he added, "Let me know what happens with that ghost of yours."

And that was that.

The boys knew they had been dismissed; knew it as clearly as if Ed Williams was old General Lee himself and they were his aides.

11

That Evening

Andy stopped in front of the Emporium a little before seven, peering through the side window to make sure the store was empty. With a sigh of relief, he saw that it was.

Andy needed to talk with Mr. Williams.

All day he had pondered the old proprietor's words. All day thinking and wondering. Wondering why a spirit would stay around after the body had given it up.

Was Heaven that hard to reach?

Or was Hell just that busy?

These are the thoughts that toy with young minds. Walking through the front door of the Emporium, he spotted Mr. Williams next to a side wall, unpacking a box of imitation Union caps that little tourist boys snatched up for $7.95 each. They sold well, too. Over a hundred a week during the busy summer months.

Ed looked up and waved.

"What's up, kid?" he said, pulling the last stack of caps from the box.

Andy fidgeted a minute, long enough to grab Mr. Williams' attention.

"What's eating you?"

"Just been thinking 'bout what you said this morning."

"What did I say?"

"You know, 'bout spirits getting lost after they die."

Ed shrugged. "Just a theory. I'm not a college professor or anything like that. I'm just a student of life. Always trying to look on the practical side and the practical side tells me that maybe spirits get lost."

He paused, looking up at Andy. "Or maybe they're just not ready for Heaven."

"What do you mean?"

Ed stood and rubbed his chin. "I just remembered something I heard when I was a kid," he said. "Our preacher, now what was his name? Corbin? No, Courtley – I think. Funny how you can't remember stuff like that. Anyway, one Sunday when I was about your age, he's up at his little podium preaching fire and brimstone, and he says something I'll never forget."

"What?"

"Hold on. I'm getting to it," Ed said, patting Andy on the shoulder. Pushing the empty hat box out of the aisle with his foot, Ed patted first one shirt pocket, then the other in search of his glasses. "Now where'd I leave those?" he muttered to himself. Shrugging, he continued. "You know what a pestle is, Andy?"

"Uh-uh."

"Well, a pestle is a tool you use to pound stuff into mortar – limestone and sand; stuff like that. Usually a pestle has a slightly rounded end and a handle. Like a weird phallic symbol."

"What's a phallic symbol?"

"Never you mind!"

"How am I supposed to know what it looks like then?"

"It's a stick with a ball at the end, all right?"

"A stick with a ball at the end. Okay. I got it."

"As I was saying, you just put your material in a bowl and grind away with the pestle until all that's left is a fine mortar."

"So your preacher told you how to make mortar?"

"No, smart aleck! I'm trying to educate you, so pay attention."

"Yes, Sir!" Andy said, saluting smartly.

"As I was saying, the preacher was up at his podium, or pulpit I guess is what you call it, and he says this. He says 'Life is God's pestle, a mighty tool with which he grinds the souls of men into a fine mortar we call faith. For only after a good grinding will faith hold strong and true.'" Ed paused and let the words sink in.

"I still don't get it," Andy said after contemplating the preacher's words. "What's that got to do with ghosts?"

Ed looked at Andy for a long moment before answering. "I was just thinking," he sighed, "that maybe there are some souls that God's not through grinding on."

It was as simple as that. Andy now understood what Mr. Williams was getting at. Nodding slowly, then looking up at the old proprietor, he said, "God didn't get a chance to grind them – to test them – like they were supposed to be tested, did he?"

Mr. Williams winked and nodded. "It's either that," he said, "or they're too damn stubborn to leave."

"I think they're too stubborn," Andy grinned.

Ed smiled. "I reserve all judgment," he said, "until God's done grinding on me. Now, you gonna stick around and help me close, or what?"

"I don't know," Andy teased. "What kind of ice cream you got?"

"Pistachio Almond."

"Okay, I can stay."

An hour later, as Andy played with his ice cream, he found that he had a spoon that looked much like a pestle – and a bowl of Pistachio Almond that mashed very nicely. When ground properly it made a cold, greenish mortar.

Life is God's pestle, Andy thought.

Grinding.

Grinding.

Grinding.

12

Later That Night

Devil's Den loomed before the boys as they glided down Crawford Avenue. The great boulders rose ominously from the evening mist – like imposing icebergs drifting silently in the frigid Arctic Sea. The wind rushing past their ears blocked out any sounds there might have been, creating a surreal world that unfolded before them like a Gothic play.

Reaching the southern elbow of Crawford Avenue, just before the asphalt looped around and headed to the northwest, the boys pulled off the road and hid their bikes where they wouldn't be spotted.

Standard procedure.

Sitting on the stone hedge outlining the parking lot, they waited for the ghost. Watchful and silent. Climbing up on the rocks would have offered a better vantage point for ghost watching, but then, there were the crevices to consider.

Great gaping holes.

They would be dark this time of night.

As one passed, it would be hard not to cast a sideways glance into such an abyss. To think that something might be looking back was more than the boys could handle.

They didn't call it Devil's Den without reason.

"Think he'll show?" Grant asked, and though his question was only a whisper, the words seemed to echo off the rocks with robust enthusiasm. Silence is so relative. Even a whisper can sound like a roar when the heart starts to tremble.

Andy shrugged.

"Bet he will," Jeff said.

"Yeah, and what do we do then?" Matt asked.

"Introduce ourselves," Jeff replied.

"Oh, sure? You're going to walk up to a ghost that's been dead a hundred and thirty-one years and just say 'Hi!'"

"I will, just watch."

Five minutes of dismal silence followed, cast against a backdrop of shadows and mist. Finally, Jeff could stand no more.

Conversation was called for.

Poking a stick absentmindedly at the pavement, he looked across at Andy. "Earlier today, at the Emporium, you said something about a colonel."

"I remember," Andy said.

"Who was he?"

"Colonel Chamberlain, Joshua Chamberlain."

"Yeah, that's him. How come you know so much about him? I mean, what's the big deal? Did he die here or something?"

51

"No. Actually he fought out the rest of the war and rose to the rank of General, Major General, I think. After the war, he went back to Maine and became Governor."

"Ohhh," Jeff mewed, nodding his head with understanding.

"That's not the reason he's special, though," Andy continued. "At least not to me. You see, the 20th Maine, that was his regiment, they were the extreme left flank of the entire Union line. If the Rebs got around the 20th Maine, it was all over for the Army of the Potomac. Chamberlain knew that and he wasn't about to let the Rebs flank him."

Standing, Andy walked out into the road until he could see the dark outline of Little Round Top in the distance. Pointing, he said, "See the monument up there that looks like a castle?"

Jeff jumped to his feet and walked out until he could see where Andy was pointing.

"Yeah, I know the castle."

"Well, that's for the 44th New York. They were the third regiment over from the 20th Maine. The 83rd Pennsylvania was between them and on the other side of the 44th was the 16th Michigan. They were the four regiments that made up the Third Brigade, Colonel Strong Vincent's brigade. Well, at least it *was* Colonel Vincent's brigade."

"What do you mean?" Matt asked.

"Vincent was killed during the attack."

"Oh."

"It was the Third Brigade that held the high ground on Little Round Top. They took some pretty heavy losses doing it, too. After a bunch of assaults on the hill, Colonel Chamberlain's men were almost out of ammunition. He knew they couldn't hold off another attack without ammo, so he ordered his men to fix bayonets–"

"Cool!" Jeff cawed.

"–and they charged down the hill."

Andy fell silent for a moment, resting his hands on his hips as he stared up at the hill.

"What happened?" Matt asked eagerly, as if he were afraid Andy wouldn't finish the story.

"Well, they came down the hill in a sweeping motion, like the arm of a pendulum. Colonel Chamberlain and his men captured something like five hundred Confederates that day and saved the Union flank."

"That's wild," Grant said.

"Yeah," Andy said, turning to look at his friends. "They gave him the Congressional Medal of Honor for it, too."

"Too cool!" Jeff said. "I didn't know anything like that happened here."

"You live here!" Andy snorted. "Don't you think you should know what happened? I mean, we come out here every Friday and Saturday night and dig up old bullets and buckles and canteens and all that other stuff we find. Doesn't it make you curious? Don't you ever want to find out more, find out what really happened? Who was fighting? Geez, Jeff! All you have to do is go to the Cyclorama to see what happened."

"I've been there," Jeff argued. "I'm just not that interested in history, that's all."

"You thought what Colonel Chamberlain did was pretty cool, you just said so."

"That's different," Jeff protested.

"No it isn't! It's history! It's exactly what all this was about. Guys like Chamberlain doing these incredible things – impossible things. History is full of stories like that. What about General Armistead?"

"Who?"

"General Armistead. He was with General Pickett when the Confederates charged the Union center across a mile of open field. It was a slaughter. Cannon blowing holes in the Reb line, musketry tearing them up. It's amazing *any* of them survived."

"What about Armistead?" Matt pressed.

"Up near the Cyclorama there's a marker where he fell – mortally wounded. He made it all the way to the Union line, actually broke through before going down. A couple days later he died. He was a pretty amazing guy, old Lo."

Looking over at Matt, Andy explained, "That's what they called him, Lo. His real name was Lewis." Pausing, he shook his head. "You know, the funny thing is that all Armistead really wanted was to see his old friend, General Hancock."

"Who was he?" Grant asked.

"A Union general. He and Armistead were friends before the war. And they were still friends, even here at Gettysburg."

"Oh, man," Matt said with a low whistle. "So like, now they were fighting each other?"

"That's right. Before saying their good-byes at the start of the war, Armistead swore that he would never raise his hand against Hancock and asked God to strike him dead if he did. When Armistead charged across that field with Pickett, it was Hancock he was attacking."

"I don't think I could handle that," Jeff mused, shaking his head sadly.

"It was like that a lot," Andy said. "Guys who fought together before the war, or were classmates at West Point, were suddenly on different sides trying to kill each other. I guess that's why so many people are interested in the Civil War; it's America's great tragedy."

"Man, that's intense," Jeff said.

Andy smiled. "History's not that bad after all, is it? You should read a real book sometime – and Playboy doesn't count!"

"Somebody's got to teach him to read first," snipped Grant. "That's why he reads girlie magazines, they're all pictures."

"I know how to read," Jeff replied with a scowl. "I just never found anything I wanted to read."

"Well," Andy said, "I've got a whole wall full of books. Anytime you want to read something good, just let me know."

Jeff flashed him a grateful smile and once again the intrepid Marauders fell silent.

Deep, mist-shrouded silence.

After a few minutes, Grant broke the still night air again. "How long we been here?" he asked.

Andy looked at his watch. "Forty-five minutes."

Again, silence.

Grant shifted uneasily. "Anyone feel like doing some scanning? I mean, we're already here. Maybe if we don't look like we're waiting for the ghost he'll show up."

"I don't feel like scanning," Matt said. "This place gives me the creeps."

"It's better than just sitting here," Grant said.

Shooting Grant a penetrating *you're-starting-to-irritate me* glare, Matt said, "No!" and the discussion quickly ended.

An hour later they mounted their bikes and left Devil's Den as fast as their legs would pedal. No ghost appeared during their clumsy surveillance and they began to wonder if maybe Mr. Williams was right. Maybe the ghost was nothing more than a figment of their collective imagination.

But Andy knew better. He knew that something *had* happened that night; he felt it. Unseen eyes had probed them from the dark mass of rocks up on Devil's Den.

Eyes that were not mortal.

He felt them as surely as if he had seen the watcher standing there on the rocks, staring at him from beyond the grave.

And then there was the voice.

Or was it a voice?

It could have been just the wind; the whispering wind.

None of the others seemed to hear it.

None of the others heard the wind whisper "I've lost m'drum."

13

Thursday, June 9

It has often been said of people who do irrational things, that there is a method to one's madness. It may not have been phrased quite that way, but the general message remains the same.

Napoleon was mad in a megalomaniac way, while Van Gogh was more creative in his madness; a man with an ear for art. Hitler was Aryan mad, and Jeff Kowalski was Geena Davis mad.

Mad.

Mad.

Mad.

There are a million varieties of madness.

The madness of Andy Martin, however, was a class unto itself. A special madness. A madness rooted in genius; cool, calculating genius.

Andy was talking with Grant in the main hall of Gettysburg Middle School. It was lunch time. It was also the last day of school.

As they talked, Grant was blissfully unaware that he was a tool in Andy's hands. A tool with a specific purpose and for a mission that Andy had meticulously planned for over a week. It was time to act. The tool was ready and in place. The weapon of choice was in Andy's hand – an innocent looking can of Diet Coke.

Grant was busy complaining about the lackluster performance of the Orioles, a team he touted as the only ball club "worth their jockstraps." He was the only seventh grader Andy knew who took it personally when a baseball team lost.

As Grant ranted on, Andy kept an eye on the far end of the hall. Watching and waiting; like a U-boat commander with his periscope riding above the waves, searching for an elusive quarry.

Patience to the hunter.

Patience to the U-boat commander.

Suddenly he was there. Target sighted. A Twinkie tanker displacing two hundred pounds and listing to starboard was dead ahead and chugging Andy's way.

Time to rack up some tonnage.

At the end of the hall, Burke Holtz strolled out of the cafeteria, breaking his stride just long enough to pick his unbrushed teeth. In his left hand he gripped a thick slice of Italian bread which he proceeded to stuff down his gullet, giving each bite the required three chews before swallowing.

As the bully drew near, Andy watched his eyes, waiting for the moment of recognition. Closer and closer Burke strolled, scowling eyes wandering from face to face as the bully consumed his self-disgust in the form of Italian bread and venomous anger.

Finally! Eye contact.

Staring at Burke with unblinking eyes, Andy leaned close to Grant and whispered, "Do me a favor. Turn around and look at Burke, then laugh like I said something funny."

Grant was mortified. "Are you crazy?"

"Just do it," Andy said between tight, smiling lips.

Grant hesitated, then quickly glanced at the approaching bully. Snorting a laugh that most would have instantly recognized as either phony or hysterical, Grant leaned close to Andy and hissed, "What are you doing?"

There was no time for an answer.

Planting his large frame in front of Andy, Burke sneered, "What's so funny?"

Grant's back was to Burke and he made sure it stayed that way. He needn't have worried, though. Burke's eyes were locked on Andy, as if by sheer force of will he could bore holes through his nemesis. They were angry, witless eyes that were too slow to recognize a set-up.

That was Burke Holtz: witless wrapped in corduroy.

"I said, what the hell is so funny?" Burke snapped.

"Nothing." Andy smiled.

"What you laughing 'bout then? Huh? I'm not stupid! I know when someone's talking 'bout me."

"We were just talking."

Grabbing Andy by the collar and pressing him against the locker, Burke's snarling face was so close that Andy was swimming in rancid breath. "You better not be talking about me or I'll get you after school, when no one's around to stop me. Ya hear?"

Andy nodded.

Snatching the Diet Coke from Andy's hand, Burke said, "Don't mind if I do." Taking four big gulps that finished off the soda, Burke crushed the can against the locker by Andy's head and let it drop to the ground. "Got a problem with that, Martin?"

"No," Andy whispered, shaking his head in feigned terror, while fighting desperately to keep from smiling.

"Good," Burke belched. Slapping Andy across the face just hard enough to paint his cheek crimson, the bully turned and continued down the hall.

"What do you think you're doing?" Grant stammered. "You just about got me pounded."

"Relax. He's not after you, he's after me. Besides, that's exactly what I wanted him to do. He's so dumb he's predictable."

"You going to tell me what you're up to?"

"Not much. I just altered my Coke a little. It won't hurt him, just turn his tongue and lips black and make him pee orange for a couple days. Oh, yeah!" Andy snorted, "I put a couple of my mom's laxatives in there, too. That should keep him in one spot for a while."

Grant shook his head in disbelief. "You're crazy. When he figures it out, he's gonna pound you. And me!"

"Today's the last day of school," Andy said with a shrug. "Unless Burke flunks eighth grade – which *is* a possibility – he'll be in high school next year and we won't see him."

Grant was still shaking his head.

"What?" Andy said with a half-smile.

Before Grant could answer, a voice bellowed from the far end of the hall, "MARTIN!"

Grant and Andy exchanged horrified looks. With their faces only inches apart, they screamed, "RUN!" and quickly took their own advice.

So much for the seventh grade.

14

Friday, June 10

The mist comes often to the hills and fields of Gettysburg, creeping in on the wings of darkness like the midnight shadows of clouds gone to rest. It hugs the ground, billowing slightly in the gentle breeze that frequents the Pennsylvania countryside.

Rising and falling with the wind, the mist lends the appearance that the earth is breathing. Shallow breaths; inhaled, then exhaled. The mist shrouds the land, as if to guard its secrets from the prying eyes of a curious world. On the darkest nights, when the moon is hidden and the stars are smothered in cloud, the mist takes on a different appearance.

It's as if those who died here breathe again, their exhaled breath frosted by chill tombs they cannot escape. If you were to walk barefoot through these fields at such a time, would you feel their breath licking at your ankles? Would you feel the fingers of a dead soldier clutching at your knee as he called to you from beyond the grave?

Dead soldiers.

Bodies broken like cheap toys. Lives never to live again; eyes never to see. They are gone, never to return. Bones confined to earthen beds with nothing but boards of rotting pine to protect them from worm-laden soil.

Gone.

From the pages of old photo albums their faces stare at us from across time. The frightened eyes of boy soldiers looking into flash cameras; moments in time captured for the folks back home. Sometimes these faces have names. Names all but forgotten now except on the monuments where they are chiseled with finality. In a thousand years even these will be gone.

But the mist will remain.

That, and the bones of the dead.

* * *

At Devil's Den, the Marauders were wrapping up another night of scanning when the ghost made its appearance. Without the fanfare of whirling mists or poltergeist-inspired chain rattling, the ghost simply materialized on the boulder next to the bridge at Plum Run, next to the bikes.

"Holy cow!" Jeff yammered. "It's it! It's it! Crap-ola, look at that! Holy cow!"

Jumping to his feet, with eyes as big as golf balls, Grant shouted into the woods, "It's the ghost! It's the ghost! It's the ghost!" Stumbling back, he looked at Jeff, then back at the ghost. For a moment it looked like he might bolt across the field. The only thing that stopped him was the death-grip Jeff had on his arm. "Don't leave me!" Jeff croaked, clawing at Grant with both hands. "My legs won't work! Don't leave me!"

On the other side of the bridge, Matt and Andy sprinted down the path, half expecting a hoax, but alarmed enough by Grant's tone to come as fast as their legs would carry them.

The ghost was between them.

It was strange to look at him, Andy thought. He didn't resemble a classical ghost, meaning he wasn't transparent. The only thing that hinted at his true identity was a thin aura that shimmered around his head.

The spook sat silently, watching them with unearthly eyes that gave only a hint of what lay beyond. Eyes that wandered from face to face. First looking at Grant and Jeff, then turning and staring curiously at Matt and Andy. It was as if he were waiting for something; a word or a gesture.

Perhaps he waited for Matt to reach into his marble bag and hand over a freshly excavated bullet – the bullet that had killed him so many years before.

He didn't say.

Andy's legs began to feel like rubber bands as he stared in silent disbelief at the phantom on the other side of the creek. No one moved, no one spoke. Even the crickets grew silent as the dead and the undead waited. It was like a wicked game of chess where the pieces are all gray and no one knows who's supposed to make the first move.

Leaning close to Matt, Andy whispered, "Come on," and took a hesitant step toward the bridge. His legs were still shaky and uncooperative; as if waiting for his disbelieving brain to wake up and scream at his muscles to *RUN*.

Adrenaline was stoking the fire in Andy's heart and the billows of fear blew the flame into a white-hot, feverish blast. Blood pulsed through his veins like air through a high pressure hose. His ears throbbed with the racing *dump-dum-dump-dum-dump-dum* of a terrified heart.

Step by step, Andy and Matt crossed the bridge, their eyes glued to the ghost who was perched on the boulder twenty feet away. Spectral eyes followed their every move. Cocking his head to one side, the ghost looked as if he were listening to the pounding roar of four hearts bursting inside their young chests.

On the other side of the bridge, Andy and Matt quickly huddled with Jeff and Grant, each vying for the position farthest from the ghost.

"What do we do?" Jeff asked as his teeth began to chatter – from the cold, he would later argue.

"I say we run!" Matt hissed.

"We can't," Grant moaned, his teeth now joining Jeff's chorus. "Ghosts can fly and walk through stuff; don't you ever watch old movies? No matter where we go, he'll block our way." Grant was shaking as he and Jeff clung to each other. "Man, we're gonna die! I just know it!"

"We're not gonna die!" Matt snapped.

"What are we gonna do then?"

No one answered.

After a long moment, Matt elbowed Jeff. "Now's your chance to introduce yourself."

Jeff didn't answer, but a strange look crossed Andy's face and before any of them realized what he was doing, he said, "I'll do it," and stepped toward the ghost.

For a moment, Andy wondered if he was incredibly brave or amazingly stupid. Every perpendicular hair on the back of his neck told him to run in the opposite direction as fast as his legs would carry him, but still he plodded forward. His legs were heavy and weak, almost non-responsive. He felt like he was wading through a swamp of knee-deep concrete.

Of all the body parts a young boy has, the legs know best when it's time to run. It's quite simple: when a bully chases you – run. When a foaming-at-the-mouth, shaved-buffalo-looking dog wants to turn you into an early lunch – run. And when a ghost sits on a rock twenty feet away and stares at you – RUN!

Still, Andy plodded forward, placing each dread footstep softly on the ground as if sneaking up on the ghost rather than greeting him. At any moment he expected the spirit to vanish, or turn into a ghoulish skeleton. Or worse yet, a blood drenched corpse.

With each step, Andy found himself closer to the spirit until, at last, they stood facing one another. Their eyes met and locked: the mortal and the immortal, the living and the dead. Andy would later recall that this was the ultimate game of blink – and he was destined to lose from the start. Only now did the young Marauder begin to realize that this was no surreal vision dancing before his eyes.

Visions pass when you blink.

Nightmares melt when you wake.

The ghost did neither.

Eye to eye, Andy's nerve was straining dangerously close to its breaking point. His mind raced through a series of escape plans and he was about to shout, "Let's get out of here!" when the ghost did something quite unexpected.

He smiled.

It was almost as if he sensed Andy's rising alarm and wanted to calm him, to ease his fear. It was an unspoken message of friendship, or at least friendly intent.

It worked.

Swallowing hard, Andy looked at the ghost, then at the Marauders, then back at the ghost.

"What's your name?" he finally asked, and as the words crossed his lips, he thought how strange his voice sounded. How hollow. As if someone had spoken the words for him. *I'm talking to a ghost,* Andy thought, and for a moment he imagined that this was all a dream and that he would wake soon in his own bed. Safe and sound on West Street.

It wasn't to be.

At first, it appeared the ghost couldn't or wouldn't respond. Then, looking up at Andy, he said, "My name is Joshua Harding. My friends call me Josh." Surprisingly, his voice was soft and pleasant, almost charming.

Andy's trepidation now melted into a pool of relief. The twitch of a smile marked the corner of his mouth as he cautiously offered his name. "I'm Andy. Andy Martin."

The ghost nodded, and though he was still smiling, his eyes betrayed a sadness he could not hide. Andy felt those eyes gazing through his flesh and into his soul. Piercing and penetrating eyes, ancient and mysterious. They were the eyes of an old spirit who was weary of seeing and now wanted only rest.

"I've lost m'drum," Josh said at length. "Do you know where it is?"

Andy shook his head. "Where'd you lose it?"

"I had it on Union Hill," Josh said with a shrug, pointing up the slope of Little Round Top.

"Union Hill?"

"Yes," Josh said, pointing once again at Little Round Top. "Union Hill, right up near the crest. Felt like an ornery mule kicked me in the head and when I woke up, my drum was gone."

"I'm sorry," Andy said. "I don't know where it is."

There was a moment of awkward silence. "You live in these parts?" Josh asked, looking at Andy's clothes with a curious eye.

"In Gettysburg," Andy replied. "How about you? Where are you from?"

"Erie."

"You were–" Andy stopped and corrected himself, "You *are* with one of the Pennsylvania regiments then, right?"

"Eighty-third Pennsylvania, Company B," Josh replied.

"Third Brigade!" Andy stammered, growing visibly excited. "Geez! Mr. Williams was right!" Looking at Matt, then back to Josh, he said, "That's Strong Vincent's brigade, right?"

"Yes," Josh replied, surprised at Andy's reaction. His smile quickly faded, and a look of suspicion crossed his face. "You're not a spy, are you?"

"No," Andy laughed. "I just love hist-"

Josh suddenly sprang to attention and turned a quarter circle away from the boys. "Yes, Sir," the spectral drummer barked crisply to the empty night air. Snapping a sharp salute, he held it for a full ten seconds. "On the southwest slope, yes Sir," Josh sang. And as the ghost continued to talk, his voice suddenly went mute. His mouth still repeated the unheard orders, but the words were swallowed by another dimension that none of them could penetrate. In fascination, the Marauders watched as Josh began to fade. First his color drained away, fading like a scrap of paper under a desert sun. As they watched in horror, his feet disappear. Then his legs, torso, and chest, swallowed by a consuming nothingness that crawled slowly up his body.

Realizing what was happening, Josh turned to Andy. He started to say something they couldn't hear, but then his mouth was gone, followed quickly by his cheeks, forehead and hair until all that remained were his eyes. Eyes that stared at Andy from beyond death and time.

Ancient eyes.

A moment later the floating orbs winked out; like stars dying in the morning sun.

No one moved.

They stood frozen in place; rock-solid-still. It was as if wicked Medusa and her wig of slithering serpents had walked the battlefield that night and turned them to stone.

The silence was soon broken by the chirping of first one cricket, then another, and another, until the sound seemed deafening. The woods, so silent and still a minute before, now stirred with the tireless hum of nocturnal ventures.

Grant was the first to break the spell. "Oh, man!" he whispered. "Oh, man! I don't believe it."

Matt was next to stir. "What was all that about? That 'Yes, Sir!' stuff he was talking at the end?"

"I'm freakin'," Jeff said, waving his hands spastically in front of himself. Stumbling over to the stone wall by the parking lot, he plopped down hard on the cool rock and began to hyperventilate.

"Oh, man! Let's get the bikes and get out of here," Grant said, trying to harden his voice and sound assertive, but failing miserably.

"Josh Harding," Andy whispered to himself, staring at the rock where the ghost sat. "Eighty-third Pennsylvania. Unbelievable."

The woods around Devil's Den were starting to take on a frightful look when Jeff and Grant decided they'd had enough for one night. With no pretense at courage they bolted for their bikes.

The funny thing about panic is that it's predictably contagious. Call it Chicken Fever. Call it Spinal Incontinence. Call it what you like. Whatever it was, Matt and Andy were soon smitten.

With anxious legs urging pedals to turn faster, the boys left the dark rocks of Devil's Den behind. The more distance between them and the haunted woods, the better. As they rode, Andy cocked his head to one side. He thought he heard something, but wasn't sure.

There it was.

A voice calling, as if from a distance.

"Andy, I've lost m'drum," it cried, but none of the others seemed to hear it.

Turning his face back into the wind, Andy rode on.

15

Saturday, June 11

The Adams County Public Library was at the corner of Baltimore Street and East High Street, two blocks from the center of town. Normally, a trip to the library would take Andy north to High

Street and then east a couple blocks to Baltimore Street, thus avoiding Duke the Killer Mongrel. But today he had to drop off a piece of errant mail to widow Deigert.

That meant Breckenridge Street.

That meant Duke.

At sixty yards, Andy saw the beast burst from behind a hedge. Snarling savagely, Duke studied Andy, his wicked eyes filled with bicycle lust. With bounding strides, the cur moved to intercept his two-wheeled adversary. Saliva flew from his curled lips as he ran, his mind intent on one thing and one thing only: Get the bike!

Like comets on a collision course, the gap between Andy and the vile dog shrank at a frightful rate.

Closer.

Closer.

At fifty feet Andy pulled the squirt gun.

At ten he used it.

Duke didn't know what hit him. With a yelp, he skidded to a halt and began pawing at his face. Shaking his head like he'd just had a bath, he turned and sprinted back to the Cole's front yard where he ran full force into a small tree. Squatting on the ground, he pawed at his face again, then ran his head through the Cole's uncut lawn to wipe the shampoo from his fur and away from his eyes.

After racing around the yard a few times, looking as if he were trying to mow the grass with his ear, Duke glared at Andy from across the yard. A wicked glare. There was a low rumble in the dog's throat, followed by a halfhearted bark, but that was it.

Andy smiled. "I guess we understand each other." Giving the dog a sloppy salute, he continued on to Mrs. Digest's.

Duke just watched him go.

There would be no chase today.

16

Parking his bike in the rack outside the Adams County Library, Andy chained his front wheel to the metal rack and raced up the Aztec-like steps to the main entrance.

"Hi, Andy," April May said with an instinctively seductive smile as Andy passed the checkout desk.

"Hi," Andy smiled, a creeping warmth rising up his cheeks. He knew he was blushing and this made him blush all the more. April May had that effect on him. Sometimes it's terrible being twelve going on twenty. So awkward and shy while at the same time so aware of passion's fire.

Of all the girls in Gettysburg, April May was the only one Andy had any interest in. She was nineteen, which presented an age problem. But she was smart, loved books, and loved the Civil War.

She moved to Gettysburg from Baltimore the year before, two months after graduating high school. In Andy's eyes she was as fresh and invigorating as the months of her name.

Fresh as spring.

Across the room, old Mrs. Bartholomew took off her schoolmarm glasses and beamed down at Andy from the top rung of a book ladder. "Well hello, young man," she cooed. "How is your summer vacation?"

"Great, so far," Andy said. "How are you, Mrs. Bartholomew?"

"Wonderful," the old woman mewed.

"How are your begonias?"

"Much better. Tell your mother she was absolutely right, as always. I tell you, that woman is a botanical genius."

"Yeah, she's pretty stuck on flowers."

"Well, what can I help you find today, Andrew? We have a new book on Vicksburg. Just came in yesterday."

"Na. I'm looking for something on genealogy."

"Genealogy? Looking up our ancestors, are we?" Mrs. Bartholomew smiled.

"No. Actually, I'm trying to find out more about some of the soldiers who fought here."

"Then you don't want a book on genealogy, per se. I think I know exactly what you need."

Leading Andy between two of the tall book islands, she scanned the shelves for only a second before spotting the tome in question.

"Here it is. Civil War Military Records." Handing the book to Andy, she said, "You should find whatever you need right here. This book tells you how to order pension records, military service records, and other information from the National Archives in Washington, D.C. All you need to know is the name and unit of the person you're researching. It is much simpler than tracking down birth certificates. In fact, I've used it myself."

"This is great," Andy said, scanning quickly through the book. "I didn't know you could get service records."

"You have to fill out a form with your request, but they have a sample in the back that you can copy. May I?" Taking the book from Andy, she flipped to the back and quickly found the page. "Here it is. Request form NATF-80. National Archives order for copies of veterans records. Just burn a copy of the sample and fill it out."

"Great!"

"See? Just ask your friendly librarian," Mrs. Bartholomew chirped. "We aim to please."

"Thanks," Andy said.

Walking up to the counter, up to April May and her full, cherry red lips, Andy pulled a well-worn library card from his pocket. April scanned the card and stamped the book before leaning over the counter and taking Andy's hand.

"Make sure you come visit me, little boyfriend," she purred. "I want to pick your brain some more."

"Sure," Andy smiled, stuffing the book clumsily into his knapsack. "See ya later, April."

Averting his eyes from her devastating figure, Andy made a beeline for the exit. With the door cocked halfway open, he turned and waved. "See ya later, Mrs. Bartholomew. Thanks again."

April watched him go, her chin resting in her hand, wishing that the guys she dated were as mature as Andy Martin. Wishing, perhaps, that she was a little younger or he a little older.

Sweet April May.

There was more than one reason Andy loved his library.

17

Friday, June 17

There is something special about turning thirteen. Something aside from acquiring that infamous nomenclature that most parents only hiss through clenched teeth.

That's right: *teenager.*

Early in their child-rearing endeavors, parents are often warned about the teenage years by concerned friends and family. These warnings often include horrifying anecdotes about so-and-so's kid who did what-all and ended up in juvenile hall.

Stories every parent needs to hear.

Of course, these stories are rarely firsthand accounts and if you brought them up later, you'd quickly discover that it wasn't so-and-so's kid after all. It was whoozit's kid. And he didn't end up in juvenile hall. He got three hours of detention at school.

Parents get confused like that sometimes.

Some believe this is due to the interference of sun spots on the parental grapevine.

Who knows.

For boys, turning thirteen is the first real step toward manhood. Soon they'll be sneaking into the bathroom to try out dad's razor. They'll try the shaving cream, slapping it on their face by the fistful until half of the white mess sags and plops into the sink. They'll cut themselves, then stick half a roll of toilet paper to their face to stop the bleeding. When they're finished, they'll slap some Old Spice on their cheeks and suddenly discover where the term *burning flesh* originated.

Thirteen.

That age when boys wait until mom and dad are gone, then grab the extra set of keys from the cupboard in the kitchen and race outside to start the car.

They won't go anywhere – usually – they'll just drive back and forth in the driveway, revving the engine now and then. In their minds they entertain the fantasy of cruising the strip with a carload of buxom cheerleaders.

Thirteen.

That wonderful age we never fully appreciate until decades later, after the world has stolen our innocence.

* * *

A birthday cake was waiting on the dining room table when Matt arrived home just before seven. Next to the cake, wrapped in Mickey Mouse paper, was a large box begging to be opened.

"Happy Birthday, Sport," Steve Jacobs said from the kitchen. Drying his hands on the towel next to the stove, he walked into the dining room and ruffled Matt's hair.

"Where ya been? I was beginning to wonder."

"We were at the fort. The guys wanted to throw me a birthday party."

"Oh. I hope you didn't have cake yet."

"Na. Well, not really. Jeff stuck a candle in a cupcake, only it was one of those really fat candles and it smashed the cupcake pretty good."

Steve Jacobs laughed.

"Well, I guess it's the thought that counts. Why don't you open your present. I've got a pizza in the oven and after that we can have some real cake."

Looking at the present, Matt said, "It's pretty big."

"Yeah."

Picking it up, he said, "It's heavy, too."

"Yep."

"You didn't stick a brick in here to fool me again, did you?"

"No, I didn't," Steve said, trying to sound indignant. "It didn't work the first time, why would I try it again?"

Matt shook the box.

His father cringed. "Don't do that. You might break something."

"Sorry."

Setting the box back on the table, Matt started to remove the paper, a process that proved time consuming. Gift connoisseurs around the world know that there are two types of people when it comes to unwrapping presents: those who tear the paper off with little regard for the safety of those around them, and those who are meticulous in their task. Those who carefully loosen every strip of tape with agonizing torpidity, often saving the paper and ribbon for future use.

Unlike most boys, Matt was the meticulous type.

With the corners of the present unfastened, he carefully pried the intermittent strips of tape from the underside of the box. Folding the paper out until it lay flat on the table, Matt turned the unmarked box over so that it was face up.

"A PULSAR 7000!" he shrieked. "Oh, man! This is the best! We've been saving for one of these."

"I know," Steve grinned. "Alice told me."

"Mrs. Martin? How'd she know?"

"Andy mentioned it to her. She said you boys have been trying to save your money, doing extra work on the weekends, so I thought, well, I thought I'd surprise you."

"This is the best," Matt said, shaking his head in disbelief as his hand roamed over the picture on the box.

"You gonna open it?"

"Sure. Do we have to put it together?"

"Batteries not included, some assembly required," Steve Jacobs replied with a smile. "Let me get my tool chest."

While his dad rummaged through the hall closet in search of the infrequently used tool chest, Matt cut the shipping tape on the end of the box and began to remove plastic bags filled with parts.

Quickly sorting the screws, washers, nuts, bolts, wires, and other miscellaneous parts, Matt laid everything out on the dining room table and was waiting patiently when his father returned with the elusive tool chest.

"Geez," Steve Jacobs said, looking at the parts laid out before him. "If I'd known it needed that much assembly, I could have gone to the hardware store and bought enough nuts and bolts to build my own. Probably would have been cheaper."

Over the next hour and a half, Matt read aloud from the instruction booklet while his dad did the screwing and the wrenching and the fastening. With patience and persistence they waded through all forty-seven steps of the assembly process.

"Now comes the test of tests," Steve said, straightening his back after stooping over the table longer than he should have. He stretched from side to side, then arched backwards. "I'm getting old," he complained.

"How old are you, Dad?"

"Thirty-five."

"Man! You are old."

"Thanks, that helps." Picking up the metal detector, he handed it to Matt. "Here, big mouth. See if this contraption works."

With detector in hand, Matt dropped a spoon onto the dining room floor. "Here we go," he said. "Countdown. Three, two, one, ignition." Flipping the red toggle switch to the ON position, the metal detector began to hum. Grinning at his dad, he said, "So far, so good."

"Don't get too confident, that hum could be a mechanical death rattle. See if it detects the spoon."

Taking two paces toward the spoon, Matt swept the eight-inch detector head from right to left over the utensil, moving at a conservative speed. Not too slow, not too fast. As it passed over the spoon, the speaker on the control box squawked noisily, then died down as the head moved away from the metal.

"Bingo," Steve said. "Maybe now you guys will have better luck at Mr. Sizemore's."

"Mr. Sizemore's?"

"Yeah. Alice told me that Andy was talking about sweeping for old bullets and stuff like that on Mr. Sizemore's property. You boys do have permission to be on his land, don't you?"

"Oh, yeah," Matt quickly nodded. "Sure we do."

"Well, let me know how it works, all right?"

"You bet."

"Sorry to ruin the party, Matt, but I've got to get some sleep. Early day tomorrow. Okay?"

"Yeah. I'm gonna go to bed pretty soon, too. Gotta meet Andy first thing in the morning."

With a wink, Steve said, "'Night, Sport," and started down the hall to his room. He was at the bedroom door when Matt stopped him.

"Dad?"

"Yeah?" Steve said, turning and looking at Matt.

"Thanks. Thanks for my birthday present. It's the best."

"So are you, kid," Steve said. "Sleep tight."

"I will."

As his father disappeared into the bedroom, Matt wondered how a man who had lost so much could still give so easily. How was it that fortune had allowed this man to be his father?

There always seemed to be something more Matt wanted to say to his dad. Emotion in search of expression.

Words in need of a voice.

They were words Matt couldn't speak – not yet. It was too awkward. Too embarrassing. When you're thirteen and the world seems to be against you, how do you say "I love you" to the one man who cares the most?

You don't.

You just say, "Thanks, Dad. It's the best," when what you really mean is "Thanks, Dad. You're the best."

Welcome to the teenage years.

18

There is an art to catching flies.

Not catching flies in the figurative sense, as in 'You can catch more flies with honey than you can with vinegar.'

No.

Really catching flies; those winged pests with kaleidoscope eyes and sticky little tongues. Those flies.

Most boys know how to catch flies by the time they're five or six. It's one of those junior macho-man trade secrets that float around the playground at recess.

In the early years, say second or third grade, a boy can find himself a social outcast if he fails to hone this skill properly. And, of course, by fifth grade catching flies becomes old hat.

Never use one hand.

This is the first rule of fly catching. The fly has a head full of eyes and will quickly dart in the opposite direction of an approaching hand.

Pace yourself.

This is the second important rule to remember. If you come in too fast, you'll spook the little bugger before you can properly lay your trap.

Rule number three? *Cup your hands.*

This is especially important if you want to catch the fly alive. Also, failure to observe this rule can result in a serious and disgusting case of bug guts on the palms of your hands.

Rule number four? *Always have a paper towel handy in case you forget rule number three.*

Those are the rules.

Andy was a master fly catcher. Like most endeavors he undertook, he practiced this art until he could perform flawlessly. Unlike most boys, his fascination with the swift fly had a practical purpose. Quite simply, Andy had a pet that loved flies.

Preferably alive.

From across the room Andy watched a fly circle the light overhead, then land on the opposite wall. A moment later the insect was airborne again, first bouncing off the window, then landing on the desk.

The week before, Andy spilled a few drops of soda next to his computer – a mess he never bothered to clean. Now, roaming in search of food, the fly quickly found the sweet spot. With its tongue working overtime on the sticky spill, the bug was distracted long enough for Andy to sneak up from behind. With his hands two feet apart, looking as if they were frozen in mid-clap, he descended stealthily upon his winged prey.

Inch by inch his hands slid up on both sides of the now alert fly. Moving slowly, almost unnoticeably, Andy began to close the distance between his palms.

He was almost ready.

When he clapped his hands together, the fly's senses would be momentarily overloaded with confusing and contradictory information. By the time the poor insect realized that the only escape was straight up, it would be too late.

And so it was.

Bringing his hands together with a fleshy *wump*, Andy trapped the confused fly between cupped palms. Holding his hands up to his ear, he heard the angry buzzing of the insect as it searched for an escape.

But there was no escape.

Like a human trash compactor, Andy closed his hands together just enough to stun the fly. Then, opening them quickly, he snatched the insect between his thumb and index finger. Andy did something next that would seem barbaric to the uninitiated – he ripped the wings off the fly. This done, he set the grounded insect inside one of his mom's china teacups on the window sill.

"Jaws," Andy called softly, rapping his knuckles on the glass case next to the teacup. "Time to wake up, Jaws. It's dinner time."

Lifting the lid off the terrarium and setting it gently on the floor next to the wall, Andy chased the wingless fly around the teacup three times, caught it, then held it tantalizingly over the open terrarium.

"Now remember," he lectured. "Chew your food before you swallow."

Carefully, he placed the fly in the 'mouth' of his only pet.

Jaws swallowed it in one bite.

There was no chewing, or gnashing, or tearing.

The voracious Jaws swallowed it in one bite because that is how the *Dionaea muscipuli* eat their food.

That's why they're called the Venus-flytrap.

Checking his watch, Andy stepped to his bedroom door and with premeditated stealth, turned the knob gently and peeked into the hall. The crack under his parents' door was dark and he could hear a raspy, pillow-muffled snore.

It was twenty after eleven, which gave him ten minutes to scale the side of the house and ride eight blocks to join the rest of the midnight gang.

With knapsack in hand he flipped off the bedroom light and opened the window. Tapping on Jaws' terrarium, he whispered, "If anyone wants me I'll be at the office."

Jaws didn't answer.

Some plants are just that rude.

19

Saturday, May 21

The parking lot behind the Civil War Emporium was deserted when Andy arrived. No sign of Matt. No sign of Jeff or Grant. A check of his watch told him it was exactly eleven thirty.

"Where are you guys?" Andy muttered.

Hopping off his bike, he walked it over to the only car in the parking lot: a 1972 Ford Pinto with two flat tires and a generous paint job of metallic rust. Popping his kick-stand, Andy leaned against the car's crumbling fender and shoved his hands deep in his pockets.

A minute passed, then two.

He checked his watch again; eleven thirty-two.

Sticking his hands back in his pockets, Andy felt the car shudder . . . or did it? Thinking there might be someone inside, he cupped his hands against the side window to block the reflection from an overhead street lamp and peered inside.

Nothing.

Shaking his head, he turned back to the empty lot and parked himself against the fender.

This time there was no mistake – the car rocked with a sharp jolt.

"What the–" Andy blurted, whirling around.

Springing from the other side of the car, Matt, Jeff, and Grant lunged across the hood. With ghoulish hands outstretched, they moaned and groaned a chorus that only the undead would appreciate.

Stumbling backwards and tripping over his bike, Andy quickly regained his feet and raised a defiant fist at the would-be ghouls.

"Gotcha!" Jeff hooted. "I think he pissed his pants!"

"That's not funny!" Andy barked.

"Yeah, you were scared. We got ya," Grant chimed in.

"We did," Matt said with arms crossed and a big smile on his face. "Should have seen your face."

"I knew you were there," Andy replied quickly.

"Oh, bull! You lie!" Jeff said.

"Uh-uh. Only you guys would be stupid enough to hide in an empty parking lot. Now can we get going?"

"Nice try," Matt said, "but we're not going anywhere until you 'fess up."

"Fat chance!"

"Chinese torture test!" Jeff cawed. "That'll change his mind."

"You can't get me to confess that way, moron! That's coercion."

"Co-what?" Jeff said, looking at Grant.

"Illiterates," Andy spewed, rolling his eyes in disgust. "I'm surrounded by illiterates."

"He's trying to talk his way out of it," Matt said, glancing at the others. "Just like he did last time."

"Well, it's not gonna work," Grant said, planting his hands firmly on his hips. Like that was really going to change Andy's mind.

"Can we go?" Andy said. "It's getting late."

Matt, Jeff, and Grant, arms folded across their chests, shook their heads in unison.

Sighing, Andy threw his hands in the air. "All right. To placate the simpletons, I confess that I was momentarily startled."

Jeff and Grant looked at Matt who thought about it for a minute and then nodded. "Good enough. And now that you're finally here–"

"I was right on time," Andy interrupted.

"–I can show you my birthday present."

Walking around to the other side of the Pinto where the bikes were stashed, Matt quickly returned with the old Navy duffel bag his father had given him years before. Unclipping the top, he folded the bag open and reached inside.

"Close your eyes," he told the Marauders.

When he was sure no one was peeking, he extracted the PULSAR 7000 and laid it on top of the duffel bag on the ground in front of them.

"Okay, open them."

Andy recognized the PULSAR immediately.

"Oh, no! Too cool," he said, kneeling next to the hi-tech instrument.

"Does this mean we can keep the money in the treasury?" Jeff asked, apparently not overly excited about Matt's present.

"That's all you think about," Grant said. "Money, money, money."

"And girls," Matt corrected.

"Money and girls," Grant nodded.

"I'm practicing for college," Jeff said with a grin.

"Come on, let's get going," Andy said. "I want to see how this thing works."

Mounting their bikes, the Marauders rode out of the parking lot and turned left onto King Street. The sad Pinto was once again alone, a decaying monument to modern technology. Its showcase was the parking lot and its gallery light was the street lamp overhead. Sadly, its only admirers were time and decay.

With drooping headlights it sat silently as the boys rode into the night, looking very much like a worn out dog that had grown too old for the chase.

20

A mist rolled silently across the road in front of the boys as they approached Devil's Den from the north. Like a great lumbering beast it paused for a moment over the road, as if having second thoughts about its destination. Then, with a shift of the wind, it continued on, paying no mind to the young men who braved the shadows of night's playground.

Laying their bikes next to the creek, the Marauders huddled around a penlight and an instruction book as Andy clicked off the operating procedures one by one. The PULSAR 7000 was much like their old PULSAR 500 with only a few modifications; and of course, much more power.

"Keep the light on the paper," Andy said with a pinch of irritation in his voice.

"Sorry," Jeff muttered, trying to steady the beam.

"Okay, I think that's everything. Jeff," Andy said, looking up, "you and Grant stay here and keep an eye out. Matt and I are going into the woods."

"What if the ghost shows up? Josh, I mean."

"Don't worry about Josh. Worry about the Rangers. Any sign of a car or truck, you come running. And no yelling this time."

"Yeah, yeah, yeah," Grant whined. "How come me and Jeff always get stuck doing lookout while you guys get all the fun. We never get to use the scanner or do the digging. All we do is sit here and get bored."

"Yeah," Jeff said, not wanting to be left out.

Andy and Matt exchanged looks.

"All right, it's yours," Andy said, handing the metal detector to Jeff. Taking off the headphones plugged into the side of the detector, he quickly fitted them onto Jeff's somewhat large head.

Without a word, Matt handed the hooded flashlight and spade to Grant, who took them with a triumphant smile.

"Here," Matt said, "you'll need this, too."

Unfastening the pouch from around his waist, he handed it to Grant. "All yours. Andy and I will wait here."

Jeff and Grant grinned at each other, then crossed the bridge over Plum Run. The forest waited for them on the other side; dark and uninviting. A shifting shadow of windswept trees.

Pausing, the pair stared into this menacing darkness of skeletal branches and rustling leaves. It always looked so easy when Matt and Andy did this. Why was it suddenly so different? Why did the wind shake the trees so much more and why did the shadows seem to dance around them? Exchanging a look of rising dread, Jeff and Grant could feel their enthusiasm draining out the bottoms of their shoes. Fighting over the flashlight, they managed to break off the protective hood and expose a beacon of light that cut through the night like an airport spotlight. Smothering the beam in his hand, Grant glared across the creek at Andy and Matt.

"It's not my fault," he hissed, as if accusations had already been made. Crouching, he searched the ground for the broken hood.

"Maybe we better let Andy and Matt do this," Jeff was saying, his eyes staring into the impenetrable darkness before them. "After all, they're better at it than we are. We'd probably miss all kinds of stuff."

Andy was watching this scene with some amusement when Matt tapped him gently on the shoulder.

"Hmm," Andy said, cocking his head to one side.

Matt didn't say a word – he just pointed.

Even before Andy turned his eyes to follow Matt's accusing finger, he knew what he would see. He felt the ancient eyes upon him.

And so it was.

Josh Harding, late of the 83rd Pennsylvania, was standing next to a tree a dozen feet away. His hands were at his side and he was smiling. It was a warm smile; a smile that spoke of recognition and friendship.

"Hi, Josh," Andy said, not quite sure how to greet the drummer boy.

The ghost nodded in reply.

"What are you doing out here?" Andy asked.

"This is where I am," Josh replied cryptically. "Forever I stay. There is no escape from the battle."

Andy was puzzled. "What do you mean?"

"You will understand in time."

Looking over to Jeff and Grant, who were still unaware of Josh's presence as they braced up their courage to enter the forest, Josh asked, "Where are your friends going?"

"They're looking for bullets and stuff from the battle. That's Jeff and Grant over there and this here," Andy said turning to his left, "is Matt."

"My pleasure," Josh said with a nod of his head.

"Likewise," Matt mumbled.

"Do you know . . ." Andy stopped himself, fearing the answer he might get.

"Do I know what?"

Andy looked at Matt, then back at Josh. "Do you know you're a ghost?"

With a smile cracking up the side of both cheeks, Josh put his hand to his mouth and started laughing. His soft chuckle quickly rolled into a deep belly laugh. Nodding his head in an exaggerated fashion, he finally managed to squeak out a "Yes" before the laugh took over again. "I'm sorry," he managed after a moment. "It just seems so odd, don't you think? Me! A ghost! And the look on your face," Josh said, shaking his head. "It was wonderful." Waving at them as if swatting away a pesky gnat, he said, "Of course I know I'm a ghost."

Alerted by the laughter, Jeff and Grant were staring at Josh from across the bridge, their jaws hanging two notches below par. Raising a hand in greeting, Josh smiled at them. With a halfhearted effort that was less than impressive, Jeff and Grant raised their hands in reply.

Waving them over, Josh said, "Is that one a slave or is he free?"

"Who?" Andy said. "Grant?"

"The little one there. The Negro."

"He's free," Andy said with a touch of indignation. Then, remembering who and what Josh was, he added, "You don't understand. Slavery doesn't exist anymore. It ended with the Civil War."

Josh nodded and the look on his face was one of sober satisfaction. "So I suppose it was worth it in the end. The bloodshed, I mean. The maimed and the dead. My life," he said, patting his chest, "so that he could live free." Dropping his eyes, he whispered, "Perhaps this is the noble purpose that lay beyond our horizon, beyond the fields of blood. That which justifies our loss." Looking up at Andy, he said, "Every cause must have a justification, a purpose."

Andy and Matt looked at Josh and felt pity.

"It was a good cause," Andy offered.

"Was it?" Josh said this with a hint of bitter sarcasm; his words were not meant to question, but to refute. After a long silence, he asked, "What year is it?"

"Nineteen ninety-four," Andy said.

Josh was visibly shaken. With a low whistle, he said, "I knew many years had passed, but I wouldn't have guessed that many."

Getting his courage up, Jeff asked pointedly, "How come we can see you so clearly if you're a ghost? 'N how come you're talking to us?"

Josh smiled. "I don't know. Usually we can't see into the mortal world–"

"We?" Andy interrupted. "What do you mean, *we*?"

But Josh continued without pause. "Perhaps God has seen my loneliness," he said, "and sent you so that we might be friends."

Jumping, as if startled, Josh looked warily over his shoulder.

"Now is not a good time to talk, nor is this a good place. Can you come back tomorrow eve? Perhaps then we can know one another better."

"Why should we trust you?" Grant snapped.

"Oh, shut up," Andy hissed at his suspicious friend. "And you, too," he barked at Jeff, who was about to speak his piece. Turning to Josh, he said, "We'll be here. Or at least *I* will."

The ghost smiled, then turned and walked toward Little Round Top. They watched him go, weaving his way through the rocky field until he simply vanished halfway up the slope.

A breeze drifted down from the silhouetted hill and for a moment, Andy would have sworn that it carried with it the pungent odor of sulfur.

A bitter taste of spent powder . . . and the fading echo of cannon fire.

Then there was silence.

Silence so complete that even the soft wind blowing through the trees grew mute in anticipation.

"What now?" Jeff asked.

"Well," Andy said, not taking his eyes off the spot where Josh vanished, "we came here to scan. No sense in wasting the night."

Turning, he looked at Jeff, then pointed to the black woods. "Go ahead! Scan."

Jeff and Grant exchanged a look of fearful solidarity. Without a word, they disencumbered themselves of the equipment and handed it back to Andy.

"No, thanks," Jeff muttered.

Grant just stared at the ground, kicking at an embedded rock that had no intention of budging.

Fitting the headphones back over his head, Andy switched on the PULSAR 7000. As he headed into the woods with Matt at his side, it occurred to him that, for the first time he could remember, no one questioned the courage of Jeff or Grant, the would-be intrepid treasure hunters.

It was enough that they stood their ground in the presence of the dead. It was enough that they hadn't run. For some, courage is a salty dish that must be eaten slowly and in small portions.

Andy understood this.

And in his own way, so did Matt.

21

Saturday, June 18

As the minute hand snapped to the top of the hour and the ancient wall clock began to chime its eight bells, Ed flipped the sign in the window over so that it read *CLOSED* in bold red. Sliding his master key into the deadbolt he locked the door and then lowered the shade.

The Civil War Emporium was officially closed.

Turning to Andy, who was behind the counter closing out the register, Ed said, "Rocky Road or Tin Roof Sundae, those are your choices."

"Tin Roof Sundae," Andy replied without hesitation. "Rocky Road has marshmallows. I hate marshmallows."

"Chocolate syrup?"

Andy winced. "Too much chocolate. Do you have any of that butterscotch left?"

Ed thought for a moment, "Yeah, I think so. At least, I don't remember throwing it out."

At the back of the store, behind a wall of shelves loaded with dust-laden merchandise, a narrow, green-carpeted staircase led up to the one-bedroom apartment Ed called home.

It wasn't much: a living room with a twenty-year old television against the far wall. A kitchen that was tidy to the point of looking unused. And a bedroom off the living room that was just large enough for a queen size waterbed and a chest of drawers made from unstained pine.

A small bookcase sat next to Ed's armchair across from the television. The lower shelves were packed with Civil War books, while the top shelves hosted a collection of knickknacks.

Two shelves of souvenirs; in the whole apartment, this was the only testament to Ed's sixty year adventure through life. There was the shilling he saved from a trip to London in 1968, and the jade elephant he purchased before leaving Korea. There were a couple of postcards – in sixty years, Ed never owned a camera – and a ticket stub from the 1978 Super Bowl.

At the front of the top shelf, resting in a brass frame, was the sixth-grade photo Andy gave to Ed the year before. Of all Ed's treasures, this was the most prominently displayed.

The only other picture in the apartment was a snapshot propped up against the back of the bookcase. It was an old photo, taken when Ed was still in the Army. With a muddy road as a backdrop and with rifle in hand, a much younger Private Ed Williams stood next to another man, both smiling like they were on their way to Vegas.

Andy never asked Mr. Williams about the photo or why it was so important. He always wondered, though. Wondered why a man who had very little to show for his life had chosen to keep an old Army picture.

Picking up the photo, Andy looked at it closely, searching for a clue. Was the man famous? Was he a relative? Or just a friend?

From the kitchen, Ed watched him in silence. Filling two bowls with Tin Roof Sundae, he opened the drawer next to the sink and pulled out a pair of mismatched spoons. Remembering the butterscotch, he rifled through the fridge until he found the old jar hidden in the back. Twisting the lid off, he peered inside – then winced and wrinkled his nose. "Well, as promised, we got butterscotch," Ed said. "Butterscotch `a la mold."

Holding the jar up for Andy's inspection, Ed opened the lower cabinet door and tossed the fungus infested jar into the garbage. In the living room, he handed Andy his ice cream and then slouched down in his chair.

"His name was Harry O'Connell," Ed said, pointing at the picture in Andy's hand.

"Who was he?"

"A friend."

Dipping his spoon into the bowl, Ed took a healthy bite. There was a pensive look on his face; the look of one carrying a weighty guilt that had grown too great to bear. He didn't speak again until he finished eating.

"Harry and I joined the Army together," Ed finally said, setting his empty bowl on the carpet next to the chair. "We graduated high school together and it just seemed right that we should go off to Korea together."

He was staring at his hands now, hands that were normally steady but now trembled slightly at the fingers.

"Harry wanted to be a general," Ed said in a thoughtful, far-off voice. Then, with a chuckle, "I remember right after we got to Korea, we were in the barracks and Harry decided he was going to promote himself. He cut out these stars from an old sheet and glued them to his shirt collar. As he's parading up and down the aisle and we're saluting him, the Captain walks in."

Andy sucked in his breath. "What did he do?"

Ed laughed. "Harry? Why, he popped to attention with the rest of us, but I could see the panic on his face. He was probably figuring they'd throw him in the brig for impersonating an officer. Anyway, the Captain's not giving anything away. His face is as blank as it could be as he walks up to Harry and looks him up and down."

"Geez. Did he have to go to the brig?"

"Let me finish the story," Ed said, holding up a calming hand. "I know how it ends."

"All right. Sorry."

Ed nodded. "Well, after looking Harry over, the Captain takes two steps back and snaps this really sharp salute. 'Morning, General,' he says. Well, Harry doesn't know what to do, so he returns the salute. With that same blank face, the Captain turns and marches smartly out of the barracks."

"Cool," Andy sighed.

"Yeah, you could have heard a pin drop as the Captain left. Then the whole place just busted up laughing. Course, Harry's still over there sweating bullets."

Ed chuckled again. "Yeah, good old Harry."

He lowered his eyes now and stared at his trembling hands. "One day, me and Harry were on patrol. Normal stuff. You know, done it a hundred times before. Slopping through the mud. Hell, we didn't even think there was any enemy in the area. Anyway, we came out into this clearing and they opened up on us. Cut us to ribbons. I let go with a couple of grenades and just kept shooting. After a couple minutes that seemed like forever, the shooting stopped and the enemy was gone. Some of 'em lay dead and the rest just buggered out. Of the twelve guys in my unit, I was the only one who wasn't wounded. Five were killed outright and the other six were shot up pretty bad, including Harry.

"I used the radio to call for help and a couple of trucks showed up about a half-hour later to pick us up. That half-hour seemed to drag on forever, like it was never going to end. I managed to wrap most of the wounds and stop some of the bleeding, but there were some pretty bad hits. Charlie Porter died in my arms as I was wrapping his head. Old Charlie. He caught a piece of shrapnel in his right eye. His whole face was a mess. Only saving grace was that he never regained consciousness.

"Then there was Harry. He was hurt real bad. After I'd seen to all the others, I sat next to him and just held him. Told him to hang on, that help was on the way. We were lucky, I guess, 'cause there was a MASH unit close by."

Ed looked up at Andy now. "It's funny, you know. It was just like on the TV show MASH. Only thing about the TV show, though, was that you couldn't smell nothing. And there was a certain smell about this MASH unit. Not sterile, like a hospital. Just . . . well, different. Earthy."

Throwing his hands in the air, he said, "Anyway, that's where they took us. As we bumped along the road, I could tell Harry was starting to slip. His breathing was getting real raspy and shallow. He'd taken one in the chest and one in the leg; nasty, bloody mess. I managed to wrap the leg pretty well, but the chest wound was foaming, which I knew wasn't good."

Shaking his head slowly from side to side, Ed's voice dropped to a whisper. "Harry lived until we reached the MASH unit, but died before they could get him on the operating table."

He sat for a moment in silence, head hanging low. Then, pushing himself out of the chair, he walked into the bedroom and opened the closet. Andy didn't think it proper to follow, but he watched Ed through the crack in the door as the old man rummaged through a pile of shoe boxes at the bottom of the closet.

After a drawn-out search, Ed stood, straightened his slacks, and walked back into the living room. In his hand was a small case, much like the case a watch or a long piece of jewelry might come in.

Ed handed this to Andy.

"What is it?"

"Open it," Ed said.

Carefully, Andy cracked the case open. As he did, his eyes went wide in surprise and his mouth fell open.

"Is it real?" he asked, holding the case out to Ed in both hands, as if it were some holy artifact he dare not drop.

Ed nodded, taking the case in hand. "The Silver Star. Awarded for valor, they said." He snorted. "Valor. The only reason I got this medal is 'cause I was the last guy standing. I got a medal and Harry got a funeral. Is that fair? Hell no it ain't fair! Harry should have gotten this medal. The best friend a guy could ask for. They give you a medal if you kill someone and they tell you you're a good soldier. A good soldier? Only thing is, nobody ever gives a medal to someone because they're just plain decent. Know what I mean?"

He looked at Andy to see if he understood and was a little surprised to see that he did.

"I keep telling myself," Ed continued, "that someday I'm going to fly out to California – that's where they buried Harry, in Sacramento – and I'm going to stick this old medal next to his headstone."

Closing the box, Ed set it on the shelf next to Harry's picture. "He was a good guy, Harry was. Like a brother. Sometimes bad things happen to good people. Maybe God just figures they're too good to have to suffer through this life."

Shrugging, he said, "Hell, I don't know. I'm just a tired old man." Picking up the remote, he turned the television on and the conversation ended.

Before leaving for the night, Andy took the Silver Star out of its case and laid it on the shelf. Ed watched him do this without objecting, he just shook his head ever so slightly and turned his attention back to the TV.

Just shy of his thirteenth birthday, Andy was still young enough to believe in heroes. But in a world that worships degradation, a world where right is often regarded as wrong, and wrong is right, Andy had never known a hero worthy of his admiration.

Until tonight.

22

To a photographer, there are certain images in this world that are best seen in black and white. The lone walnut tree with its empty tire swing offers up such an image as it reigns silently over a waving field of wheat. Does she wait for the children to swing and play around her trunk? Or, eagerly, does she await the reaper – to harvest away the wheat from her roots?

Black and white.

On a park bench in downtown Madrid, an ancient Spaniard frowns mournfully as he gazes upon progress at its most vile. A cough of exhaust spews fumes from a passing bus and litter blows freely in the Mediterranean wind.

After the shutter has closed, does a tear run down the old man's face? Does it stain the walkway at his feet? Or does it wash away a small corner of society's filth?

These are images that burn themselves into the fleshy walls of our mind, a white-hot brand that sizzles and scars. When captured in black and white, the mark from this mental brand can last a lifetime.

Photographers know this secret.

Some, like Ansel Adams, are masters at seeking out such images. They are men and women who, with the click of a shutter, record the history of mankind and Mother Earth.

A photographic history in black and white.

Such an image waited now.

Silent in the gathering mist.

It waited next to a bridge.

The haunting image of a Union drummer boy who carried the loneliness of too many decades upon his brow.

He was a drummer without a drum.

A spirit without rest.

Tonight, sadly, there would be no photographer to capture his image.

Josh was waiting next to the bridge at Devil's Den when the Marauders crossed the last cattle guard on Crawford and pulled off to the side of the road. When they were fifty feet apart, Andy waved at Josh, who promptly waved back, saying, "I thought you might have reconsidered."

"No way," Andy said.

It was a typical greeting between young boys, made odd only by the fact that one of them had been dead longer than Abraham Lincoln.

"What is this device you ride?" Josh asked, pointing at Andy's dark blue Huffy.

"It's a bicycle."

Josh brightened at this. "I have heard of this machine," he said, his curious eyes devouring the bicycle from axle to axle. "I've never seen one, though."

"This is how we get around," Andy said.

Josh nodded his understanding but seemed puzzled. "Wouldn't you rather have a horse? I mean, this device is splendid, but it's somewhat impersonal, isn't it?"

"What do you mean?"

"Well, it can't respond when you call its name, can it? And you can't pet it or let it eat an apple from your palm. I had a horse back in Erie, his name was Jupiter, and I rather enjoyed feeding him apples. We'd pick them from the orchard behind the house and eat them together, Jupiter and I. He was like a friend."

"Yeah, but horses are a lot of trouble to take care of."

"When a horse is your friend you don't look on his grooming and feeding as a chore, it's more like sharing. Jupiter was never any trouble, and I could always count on him for a nuzzle when I was in poor spirits. When I was twelve, I made a journey to my great-uncle's by myself. Mother was fitful about the whole thing, but she let me go nonetheless. It was two days there and two days back and it was the first time I was ever away from home. During the day it was fun, there were no adults around and I could make an expedition out of my journey. At night, however, I slept out-of-doors, which is a dreadful endeavor when you're alone, I can assure you. But I never felt alone because Jupiter was always right there beside me."

"Cool," Andy said. "My parents would never let me go off by myself."

"Some of my greatest adventures were with Jupiter," Josh said with a sad, reminiscent smile. "I miss him terribly."

"Can I ask you a question?" Andy ventured.

"Of course."

"Well, we were just wondering what you're doing here, out in the woods, and all? You seem too nice to be a haunting ghost."

"I thank you for that!" Josh laughed. "Haunting indeed! You'll soon learn, my friend, that it's the dead who are haunted, not the living. We are haunted by events we cannot change, try as we might. What am I doing out here you ask? Simple." The look on Josh's face now soured and the sadness seemed to return. "I am a pawn on God's chessboard," he said quietly. "And the Almighty knocks me about as if He were a fool who has forgotten the rules."

"You can't call God a fool!" Matt piped in, amazed that anyone would say such a thing.

Josh looked at Matt with piercing eyes. "Why not?"

"You just can't. You'll make Him mad."

"Too late, my good friend. He has already shown me His wrath. If you want to know why I am still here, ask God. It is His doing, not mine."

"At least you're not in Hell," Matt offered.

Josh shook his head slowly and stared at the ground. In a soft voice that was barely audible, he said, "You don't know. Hell is all around you and you can't see it." Turning anxiously toward Little Round Top, he hissed, "Look about you, my friends! We are on the chessboard and the game is a-play!" With the echo of his words still in the air, Josh vanished. Dissipating to a fine mist until nothing remained but the shadow of his image upon their minds.

A pawn had been played this night, but to what purpose the boys were still unsure.

23

Sunday, June 19

> *Midnight shadows upon the wall,*
> *A sense of floating as we fall.*
>
> *Rattling chains and a ghostly moan,*
> *Of such things our dreams are sewn.*
>
> *These are visions trapped in our heads,*
> *Just like the goblins under our beds.*
>
> *A well-slept night to me is rare,*
> *With thoughts as these, sleep – do I dare?*

It was 3:25 in the morning when Andy suddenly sat straight up in bed and looked around the room. He felt no fear, just the keen awareness that something uncommon had startled him from a sound sleep. A rare event indeed for a boy who slept as soundly as Andy.

Was it a loud noise?

Maybe. But the house seemed quiet now.

A bad dream, then? A nightmare that chose not to linger in the conscious mind for fear of being dispelled? Again, this was possible, but Andy felt no anxiety. He didn't feel that anxious alertness that occupies our mind after a nightmare, even when we can't remember what it was that frightened us so greatly.

Perhaps it was the falling sensation.

That straight-down-from-a-thousand-feet, in-your-gut falling sensation that ends with a jolt of wakefulness. But that sensation usually paid its visit shortly after the Sandman blew his dust, not in the middle of the night.

No. It was something else.

Something more subtle.

"Andy," came the voice.

Startled, Andy jerked his head to the left and saw a figure in the shadowy corner of his room. Before he could spring from his bed the phantom stepped forward, into the moonlight, and Andy recognized the cause of his interrupted slumber. Exhaling deeply, he patted his heart like one who has had a terrible scare.

"Josh?" he sighed in relief. "What are you doing here?"

The ghost stepped closer and it was then that Andy noticed a peculiar difference. For the first time since meeting Josh, he looked like a real ghost.

Transparent.

Vaporous.

He didn't look like the ghost Andy and the others had come to know. At Devil's Den he looked like any other fifteen-year old boy in town.

No longer.

Now he was a *bona fide* ghost.

Casper in a uniform.

Stepping to the side of the bed, Josh looked down and came directly to the point of his nocturnal visit.

"Are you my friend, Andy?" he asked.

Surprised at the question, Andy quickly replied, "Yeah. Of course I'm your friend."

Josh smiled and stepped back into the shadows. "It's lonely, you know? Not having any friends. All mine are in Heaven. Well, most of them anyway."

Andy tossed his covers back and pushed himself out of bed. "Why don't you join them, then?"

"I told you we can't," Josh replied with a shake of his head. "God won't let us. We are cursed and forsaken."

"*We?* You're talking like there are others."

"There are."

Andy was shaken by this revelation. "You're kidding! How many? Where are they?" Jumping out of bed and springing to the window, he pointed toward the battlefield. "Are they out there? Out on the field? Is that who you were talking to the other night?"

Josh didn't answer right away, but moved farther into the shadows until it was all Andy could do to see him.

"I will show you in time," Josh said. "There is a portal between our two worlds, between the living and the dead. I'm not sure you can pass through it yet. I'm not even sure if it will be there on the 'morrow."

"Let me try!" Andy said excitedly.

"Not yet," Josh said firmly, holding his hand out – as if that alone would stop Andy. "Be patient. You don't know what you're dealing with, and much as I want your friendship, I won't cheat you out of your life by letting you be trapped in the afterworld. There is something special about you. I believe that is why I was drawn to the rocks in search of my drum. So that I would find you."

Josh paused now, leaning forward into the moonlight so that Andy could see his eyes. "You have a glow about you, my friend," he said. "None of the others have it, only you. You have been chosen for a special purpose and I wish to be there when it transpires."

Josh was fading now, melting back into the shadows.

"When will I see you again?" Andy said, stepping into the shadows after him.

"Soon."

Almost as an afterthought, Andy blurted, "Will you teach me to play the drum?"

Josh flashed him a warm smile. "Happily," he said, then shrugged. "But mine is lost, remember?"

"I'll get one," Andy said quickly.

But the mist that was Josh had already vanished.

24

Monday, June 20

It was only two short weeks before the Fourth of July would swing around for its annual visit to planet Earth. It was a date that represented nothing more than a specific place in our celestial orbit around the sun. An intersection in space that's easily missed. One day it's there, the next – *BAM* – you've missed your turn and the next thing you know you find yourself at the intersection of July 5th and Eternity.

To most of Earth's inhabitants, the Fourth of July is no more important then, say, the seventh of March, or the twenty-ninth of October. But to those men and women who call themselves Americans, the Fourth of July is a very special time indeed. For on that night, across the country, the sky dances and shimmers as the patriotic celebrate the birth of a great nation.

A nation conceived in liberty and born of fire and blood. A nation that now served as a symbol of freedom for the whole world, an icon of virtue and justice.

The first week of July was a busy time of year for Gettysburg, and not just because of the Fourth. It was busy because in 1863, on the first, second and third day of that month, the small town played witness to a great struggle. A struggle that threatened to destroy that which liberty had conceived. How ironic that on the day after this pivotal battle ended, the United States celebrated its eighty-seventh year of independence.

Fourscore and seven years.

Ironic, yes.

But irony runs deep in the veins of Gettysburg.

Deep and red.

*   *   *

Mr. Williams was perched precariously on an unstable aluminum ladder when Andy rode up and parked his bike next to the double doors at the Emporium's entrance. A row of small flags already decorated the upper face of the Emporium and Mr. Williams was now trying to string a line of red, white, and blue streamers across the tops of the windows.

He wasn't having much luck.

"Need some help?" Andy asked as he watched from the sidewalk, cupping a hand over his eyes to block the sun's glare.

"I almost got it," Mr. Williams said.

He didn't.

"Want me to hold the ladder?"

"Please. This thing's so flimsy I'll probably fall and break my neck before the day's through. I might as well be on stilts."

With a wagging finger, Ed lectured, "When I was a boy, people took pride in their work and the result was a quality product. Not this flimsy trash they sell you today."

"This is kind of like that 'walking through two feet of snow to get to school' thing isn't it?" Andy said.

Looking down, Mr. Williams was about to say, "Don't be a smart aleck," when he realized Andy was right. Grinning, he said, "Yeah, I guess it is."

It was a few minutes before eleven and the thermometer on the corner of the Emporium was already pushing into the nineties. This sweltering heatwave didn't help improve Ed's opinion of meteorologists.

Like most people, Ed knew this was somehow their fault.

Resting a moment at the top of the ladder, Ed pulled an already wet handkerchief from his back pocket. Hanging onto the shoddy aluminum death-stilts with his free hand, he ran the handkerchief across his forehead and down both cheeks. Trying to ring it out, but squeezing only a few drops loose, he wiped under his chin and around to the back of his neck.

"Damn heat," he muttered. Wringing out the handkerchief again, he stuffed it back in his pocket.

Almost every day this June, the humidity level pushed past bearable and raced on toward miserable. A soup of heat and moisture that seemed to cling to every inch of the body.

Hot and humid.

Another Pennsylvania summer.

Ed pulled a staple gun from the worker's apron around his waist and tried to attach the streamers. Unlike the ladder, Ed's staple gun was made back when "people took pride in their work and the result was a quality product."

As usual, the gun jammed.

So much for quality.

Throwing a few vulgarities at the uncooperative tool, Ed loosened the gun's back catch. As he did so, the loading spring shot between his perspiring fingers and bounced off the sidewalk below. A comb of fifty-seven quarter-inch staples quickly followed, shattering and scattering on the hard concrete.

Growling, Ed stormed down the ladder.

Andy scrambled to pick up the staples, but Ed stopped him, saying, "Just leave them where they are. Maybe the moron who designed this stapler will come by and step on them."

Standing at the bottom of the ladder, Ed calmed himself, then looked up at his handiwork. "Flags look pretty good, huh?"

"They look great!"

"I've got a big one I'm going to drape over the front door, dress things up a bit."

"You want help putting it up?"

Ed shrugged. "I think I've had enough for one day. Maybe tomorrow." Wiping his mouth, he said, "I've got some lemonade in the fridge. What do ya say?"

"Did you make it?"

"No, Clair dropped it off earlier this morning."

"Then I'd love some."

"Now what's that supposed to mean?" Ed said with indignation. "My lemonade ain't good enough for ya?"

"I'd rather suck the lemons," Andy said in a matter-of-fact tone.

Ed thought about this a moment.

"Too tart?"

"Way!"

"Hmm," Ed mused, rubbing his chin as he pondered this. He didn't say it, but this was quite a blow. After all, Ed prided himself on his fresh squeezed lemonade.

"Don't worry," Andy offered, realizing that Mr. Williams was upset. "You make the best iced tea in all of Adams County."

"Sun tea," Ed beamed. "The best."

The air-conditioning was humming inside the Civil War Emporium when they walked through the door. Instantly, their damp clothing became cool and clammy, clinging to their skin like leeches on a blood sausage. It felt wonderful, though.

Inviting.

Invigorating.

Behind the counter, Ed grabbed two semi-clean glasses from the top of the miniature refrigerator.

"Ice?"

"Sure," Andy replied.

Dropping three cubes in each glass and topping them off with Clair-made lemonade, Ed sat in his chair behind the counter and pushed one of the glasses across to Andy. "Cheers," he said, then drank down the entire glass in one tip.

"Oh, my! Good! Good! Good!" Ed said, smacking his lips. "That Clair makes one good glass of lemonade. Think I'll have me another."

Taking a long cool drink, Andy's eyes scanned the open page of an immense book lying on the counter. "What's this?"

"Almost forgot about that," Ed said. "Customer brought it in yesterday. Wanted to sell it. It looked interesting so I gave him a couple bucks for it."

"A couple?"

"Okay, a buck."

"That's what I thought," Andy smirked.

"It's just a collection of old newspaper articles, New York Times, stuff like that. It makes for some pretty good reading, though. Not that I've had a lot of time for that lately," he added, lifting both hands as if to encompass the Emporium. "Guess I'm one of those guys whose work has taken over his life."

"Newspaper articles, huh?" Andy said as he flipped through the book.

"Yep. You can sure tell they didn't have *CNN* back in 1863. All the reports are at least a day old, if not more. And rumors! I was reading an article this morning, dated the third or fourth of July, said that General Longstreet was killed."

"Uh-uh!" Andy groaned in disbelief.

Taking a quick drink of his lemonade, Ed nodded as he swallowed. "That's what it said. Made it sound like it was firm as concrete. 'The rumor of Longstreet's death is confirmed' they said. Or something like that. It's nice to know that the quality and accuracy of the media hasn't changed in the last century." He took another drink. "Bunch of self-serving, liberal snakes," he muttered behind his glass.

"Who?"

"The media. They're a bunch of elitist, self-serving snakes."

"Self-serving snakes!" Andy chimed.

"Never become a reporter," Ed said, wagging a finger at Andy. "Or a politician," he quickly added. "Soon as you turn your back on them they'll sneak up and bite you in the hind cheek and then lie to you like you were their sweetheart." With his finger wagging like a berserk toll gate, he repeated, "No reporting and no politicking. Remember that."

Saluting, Andy bellowed, "Yes, Oh Captain, my Captain," quoting Ed's favorite line from *The Dead Poet's Society*.

The aging proprietor of the Civil War Emporium just smiled at his young protégé and lifted his glass in salute. "Carpe diem."

"Carpe diem," Andy grinned. "Seize the day."

After another round of lemonade, Andy walked to the back corner of the Emporium and stared up at the little Taiwanese drum tucked away on the shelf. At one time, a price tag was attached to the side of the drum. Somewhere, somehow, it had been misplaced, much like the drum itself.

Ed watched silently from the front counter.

"How much do you want for the drum?" Andy finally asked, glancing over his shoulder.

Ed pretended to ponder this question a moment, then, with a wave of his hand, he said, "Take it. It's just taking up space."

"No." Andy shook his head adamantly. "I'll pay for it."

"Come on, Andy. Just take it. The thing's been sitting on that shelf for two years."

"How much?" Andy persisted.

He could see that Ed was vexed at his stubbornness. He only strummed his fingers when he was vexed.

"I'll make you a deal," the old man offered. "Just keep helping me close, like you've been, and the drum's yours. We'll consider it payment in full. Deal?"

Andy smiled. "Deal."

Searching around the store for his step stool, Mr. Williams retrieved the dusty drum from the shelf and handed it down to Andy. "Wait," he said, holding a commanding finger in the air as he fumbled for something on the shelf. "Don't forget the sticks."

"I think I'll take it home and clean it up," Andy said, running his hand over the dusty face of the drum. "I'll be back to help you close though, okay?"

"Take your time."

As Andy started up the street, Mr. Williams watched him from the side window, a smile on his face. Shaking his head slowly, he walked back to the counter and picked up his lemonade.

"Carpe diem," he said to the empty Emporium, then downed the last of the nectar.

25

In great deeds something abides. On great fields something stays. Forms change and pass; bodies disappear; but spirits linger, to consecrate ground for the vision-place of souls. And reverent men and women from afar, and generations that know us not and that we know not of, heart-drawn to see where and by whom great things were suffered and done for them, shall come to this deathless field, to ponder and dream; and lo! the shadows of a mighty presence shall wrap them in its bosom, and the power of the vision pass into their souls.

— Major General Joshua Chamberlain
Gettysburg, October 3, 1889

Friday, June 24

"**W**here are we going?" Andy asked as the Marauders followed Josh through the rocky field at the base of Little Round Top. The ghost drummer, who was a dozen yards ahead of them, pointed to the crest of the hill, but said nothing.

On they trudged.

"Why can't we just take the road?" Grant grumbled quietly, stumbling over a boulder and almost falling.

"Shhh!" Matt hissed. "Josh knows what he's doing."

"Then what's this big secret he wants to show us?" Jeff demanded. "Why can't he just tell us, instead of being so spooky?"

"It's a surprise," Matt said, shrugging. "I don't know. Just wait and see."

They marched past the monument to the 16th Michigan and continued up toward that of the 44th New York before veering right. A dozen yards from the block which marked the right flank of the 83rd Pennsylvania, Josh stopped.

Hunkered on the ground next to him was a dim mass that shouldn't have been there. The darkness of the woods was interrupted by the shadow of something resting between the trees. As the Marauders approached, they saw that it was a tent.

A Union wall tent.

Josh was holding the front flap open.

Grant was exasperated. "What? This is the big surprise? A tent!"

"Yeah," Jeff chimed in. "Come on, Josh. We can see a tent anytime we want. What's the big deal?"

"Not a tent like this," Josh cautioned them. "No. This tent is not of your world, it is a portal between your world and mine."

Grant recoiled, stepping back several paces as if confronted by a snake. "You mean, like, that's how you got here? That's why we can see you so clearly instead of you just being all misty and ghostly?"

Josh nodded.

Andy was the only one who didn't seem surprised.

"How does it work?" Matt asked. "Do you have to go inside?"

"That is how it works for me," Josh replied. "I don't even know if it will allow your passage, but that is why I brought you here. So that if you wish, you might see my world. See sights that no mortal has ever seen. But be warned, it may be dangerous."

Matt crossed his arms. "How?"

"I don't know," Josh said, dropping the flap and stepping toward the boys. "I am afraid for you, though, because you are of the mortal world. If you were to be trapped in the spirit world I don't know if I could get you back."

"But you want us to try, don't you?" Andy said.

"That is not my decision. All I can say is that a powerful adventure waits for you on the other side."

They were silent for a moment. Eyes wandering from face to face while their young minds toyed with thoughts – with fears –

best kept private. As a breeze rippled through the trees, the acidic smell of gun powder wafted past Andy's nose. He sniffed the air, filling his lungs deeply before exhaling. "Can you smell that?"

"Gunpowder," Jeff stated.

"Were the re-enactors out here today?" Matt asked, hoping the answer was yes. Hoping, because if it wasn't, they were smelling gun powder that was spent over a century before – and that couldn't be.

Josh glanced across the slope of Little Round Top, his eyes tracking objects that weren't there, as if he could see what they could not. For a moment he looked shaken. "There is battle tonight," he stated. Before they could question him, he urged them on. "Hurry! Make your decision! We must move from this place."

"You're freakin' me out," Grant said.

"Hurry!" Josh repeated, almost frantic this time.

"I'm going," Andy stated without hesitation.

"Wait a minute," Jeff said. "What if you can't get back?"

"I will."

"You don't know that. It might be like on *Poltergeist* where the ghosts sucked the little girl into the TV and trapped her. They had to call that little short lady to get her out."

"You're such an idiot," Matt snapped, punching Jeff's arm none too lightly.

"Knock it off you guys," Grant hissed. "What if Jeff's right? What if we can't get back?"

"He's not and we will!" Matt said. "I'm going."

"No way," Jeff said, throwing his hands in the air. "This is too much." Pointing angrily at the tent, he fumed, "I'm not going in no creepy ghost tent. I don't care what you say."

"Fine," Andy shot back. "Grant, you stay here with Jeff. Me and Matt are going."

"Uh-uh! I'm going with you," Grant said, giving Jeff a sideways glance.

"Well, then," Andy said, hands on his hips, "who's going to stay here and hold Jeff's hand?"

Josh was pleading now. "We must go now or not at all. There is no more time." Without waiting, he stepped into the tent and disappeared. One minute he was there, the next minute he was gone. No fade to black or shimmer of ghostly vapor; he just vanished.

Hesitating only a moment, Andy grabbed the flap and stepped to the front of the tent. "Come on," he said over his shoulder. "Let's go!" Stepping into the tent, he vanished.

Matt and Grant quickly followed and that left only Jeff. A moment alone in the eerie woods was all it took to convince him that it was best to take his chances with the tent.

As Andy stepped through the flap, he was suddenly wrenched forward by an incredible force that embraced him and pulled at every pore of his body. Though he couldn't see anything, he felt as if he were flying through a confined space – as if defying gravity and falling horizontally through a pitch black drain pipe. A moment later the force diminished and he found himself once again standing inside the tent. Pushing the flap aside, Andy walked out into a world that was wholly different from the one he left behind – yet still the same.

The hill was still there, and the trees and the monuments. Even the roads were the same. But everything was lighter. Bright, but not a sunlit brightness.

Once, several years before, Andy had the opportunity to look through a pair of night vision goggles. That surreal glow is what now sprang to mind. As if the night was still out there in all its darkness, but somehow he could see through it. The menacing shadows that surrounded him before entering the tent now melted away to reveal a simple hill and a stand of trees.

Josh was standing nearby with a broad grin on his face. "Welcome!" he said, obviously pleased that the tent worked for the living as well as the dead. Before Andy could reply, Matt popped out of the tent and stumbled into him.

Grabbing Andy by the shoulder, Matt stared at the strange sky and the eerie forest. "Too weird! It's like the lighting at a nighttime football game, only not as bright."

A moment later Grant appeared, followed by Jeff, who quickly patted himself down to make sure that everything came through in one piece.

"Is this Heaven?" Matt asked, but any answer was quickly lost as Grant pushed his way past them and pointed frantically down the hill. Fear was in his eyes when he turned and shouted "Look! Oh, my God! Look at them!"

The others edged forward, feeding on Grant's terror, anxious for a look. Only Josh remained unmoved, staring at Grant with a stern look, "We don't use God's name recklessly here," he lectured, "You'll do well to remember that."

His words went unheeded. Awestruck, the Marauders stumbled forward en masse and stared in stunned silence at a scene they never imagined they should see.

"Unbelievable," Matt whispered.

Andy was shaking his head. "This can't be. It can't be!"

But it was.

With eyes wide and mouths agape, the Marauders stared down upon a secret that had festered upon the wounded hillside since before their grandfathers were born.

A wound that cut the land deeply and refused to heal.

A secret shared only by the dead.

26

"Quick," Josh urged. "We must find higher ground. They will be at our heels any moment." Giving Andy a gentle but demanding pull up the hill, Josh took the lead and hurried them around and behind the hill's many boulders. Climbing to the crest, he paused long enough to point down to Devil's Den. "Watch! They'll sweep around to our left. They've done it before."

But there was no time to wait and watch. With an urgent voice, Josh moved them on. Following a path just below the crest of the hill, they traveled a few hundred feet before a voice stopped them cold.

Cold like the touch of a dead hand on one's shoulder.

Cold like a tomb.

"Stop and be recognized!" the voice barked. From the shadows stepped a Union sentry, mud-stained and weary. Despite his fatigue, his rifle was steady. Its bayonet danced menacingly in front of Andy's belly.

Andy, Matt, Jeff and Grant threw their hands into the air, petrified at the sight of the bayonet-wielding soldier.

"They're with me, Jefferson!" Josh said, stepping between Andy and the bayonet. "They've come over from the other side."

"Josh?" Jefferson said, squinting hard at the drummer. "Didn't recognize ya!" Smiling now, the sentry spit on the ground near the drummer's feet. "Boy, you gonna get yourself kilt sneaking around like that. Like ta scare me ta death. Don't ya know the Rebs are on the move?"

"I know. We just saw them. Looks like they're gonna try flanking us to the south again."

Andy leaned close to Josh and whispered, "Is he a ghost, too?"

"What's that ya say?" the sentry barked.

Josh shot Andy a mischievous grin, then looked at Jefferson. "He wants to know if you're a ghost."

The sentry started cackling. "Why sure I'm a ghost. We're all ghosts here, boy." Wiping his sleeve across his mouth, Jefferson said, "Now, you best be moving back with the others. Find yourself a rock to hide behind 'til it's over."

"We will," Grant muttered. "A big rock."

Spying Josh's empty hands, Jefferson shot the drummer an accusing glare. "Say, where's your musket? Didn't lose it again, did ya?"

"Abraham has it."

"Good, good. Now you get a move on. Those Rebs are gonna come screaming through here any minute."

Running along a worn path, Josh stopped next to a boulder perched on a small rise. "Take cover here," he ordered, hurrying them behind the rock. Except for the trees, this vantage point offered them an almost unobstructed view of the carnage that was rolling their way.

To the southwest the land rippled and bulged, convulsing with the movement of men. Soldiers clad in the dusty gray of a nation that died over a century before. On they came, up the southwestern slope of Little Round Top. Halfway up they turned and swept around to the east.

"Unbelievable!" Andy said as he stared at the advancing troops.

"Believe it," Josh replied. "For here is the secret of eternal life. On the battlefield of our death we fight a war we can never win. Every night brings attack and counterattack; blood and bullet; skirmish and melee; and still the fighting goes on. Here, we dance with death every night while your world sleeps in peace."

Matt stared at Josh in awe. "You mean you've been fighting here since you died?"

"Every night. Without fail."

"How?" Andy asked. "This can't be. When you die you're supposed to go to Heaven – or something! I don't understand."

Josh forced a smile. "There is nothing to understand. Nothing at all. For us, this *is* eternity. We must fight here until the battle has been decided."

A volley of musketry erupted from the woods to their left – the furious roar of Union troops pouring their hate upon the advancing Rebels. The air pulsed as cannon began to belch their sacrilegious song. Men screamed and fell as shot and shell filled the air with a lethal breath of shrapnel.

The Rebs kept coming.

The fight now broke from the trees and the Marauders could see the action up close for the first time. Soldiers exchanging rounds at a dozen yards, some crouching to fire, others lying prone. A few stood, brazenly facing the murderous storm of lead that was bearing down on them like horizontally blown sleet.

Gazing at this whirling mass of men locked in battle, Jeff suddenly screamed, "No! They just stuck that guy with a bayonet! Did you see that?" Now, in horror, "Look! Look! He's trying to get to that rock." Jeff watched transfixed as the Confederate attempted to crawl out of harms way, his hand over his stomach to keep his intestines from spilling out. A few feet from the sanctuary of the boulder, a Union soldier approached the Confederate and calmly put a bullet in the back of the dying man's head.

The color drained out of Jeff's face and for a moment he looked like he was going to be sick. Slouching down, he turned away from the fighting.

"Be ready!" Josh barked. "We may have to move if they get any closer." Peering over the top of the rock, his hand reached for the knife at his belt before remembering that he left it with Abraham. "No knife, no musket!" Josh hissed through clenched teeth, hammering the rock with his fist.

The high-pitched shriek of an incoming Confederate shell rose above the clamor around them. Seconds later a nearby tree exploded as the shell struck, shattering the thick trunk and sending Andy and the others scrambling.

"Back! Back!" Josh shouted, pointing north as he herded them away from the rock.

Stumbling through the trees, Andy could hear minie´ balls clipping through the branches above; whistling their eerie tune as they raced through the air on their mission of death. Tumbling through the night in search of bones to shatter, in search of blood to spill.

Glancing up, a leaf came floating down and struck Andy softly in the face. Punched through its center was the jagged silhouette of an errant round.

Josh was frantically searching for someplace to hole up; someplace to take refuge until the battle was over. The last thing he could afford was to have his mortal friends fall into enemy hands.

The Rebs weren't kind to prisoners. Josh knew this with a certainty. Forty-seven times he had fallen into their hands. Sometimes he stayed in irons for a day, sometimes for a month before being bartered back. Forty-seven times the prisoner and not once had he been granted mercy. Hate makes one thirsty for revenge. It's a terrible thirst, often quenched at the expense of enemy prisoners.

"Over there!" Josh yelled, pointing to a shallow gully to their right. Scrambling over the rocks and weaving through the trees, they made their way to the natural trench and jumped in. For Grant and Jeff it was more like a dive.

Head first.

Crouching in the trench and peering cautiously over the lip, the Marauders watched as Federal troops surged forward in an attempt to push the Confederates back.

The Rebel line held firm.

The rattle of musketry shook the air in a barrage of thunder that was maddening. It was a relentless roar. Like a blast of fire from Hell's kitchen.

Piercing the air with a hideous scream, a Union soldier staggered toward them, holding the mangled stump that used to be his right leg. Fear and pain danced as one in his eyes. Just before he reached the trench a minie´ ball caught up with him, slamming into the back of his head and knocking his cap to the ground in front of the boys. Going limp, the soldier wavered, then crumpled to the ground.

Andy stared at the soldier's upturned face. It was a face that would haunt him; dead eyes staring into emptiness.

With a yell that drowned out the roar of musketry and artillery, the Federal troops pushed against the Confederate line in a second wave. This time, the Rebels gave ground. Riding on the inertia of their assault, the Federal soldiers continued the push, driving the Rebels back down the slope of Little Round Top. Fighting hard for every foot of ground, but pushing on nonetheless until the Rebel retreat was a complete rout.

The Federals were swarming around the base of Devil's Den before the murderous fire of the Confederate reserves tore into their scattered ranks. Taking shelter among the rocks, the fleeing Confederates turned and engaged the enemy, halting the Union advance and driving them back. Retreating up Little Round Top, the Union troops cheered and congratulated themselves.

Tonight was theirs.

27

Sitting near the warming flames of a bonfire two hours later, Andy poked absently at the fire with a smoldering stick. His mind played with the possibilities of what was once inconceivable.

"How many are there?" Andy asked in a soft voice.

"Four hundred and thirty-seven," Josh replied.

"Union and Confederate?"

"No, that's just Union. We don't know for sure how many Rebs there are. But it's somewhere 'tween four hundred fifty and four hundred seventy. We tried counting 'em once, but it's impossible. And ya can't believe the prisoners. They tell all kinds of tales."

Josh chuckled softly. "We had this one fella, tried to convince us that the spirit of Robert E. Lee himself had come back. That he was gonna lead the next attack."

Andy looked up.

"He didn't," Josh stated.

Andy nodded. "That would have been something, huh? General Lee back at Gettysburg."

They stared at the fire in silence for a while, mesmerized by the flame. It's funny how fire can take on new importance after one witnesses battle close up. The kiss of the flame is what starts every bullet on its crimson mission. A farewell kiss of death. A quick peck on a black powder cheek.

Fire.

Man's greatest discovery.

And at the same time, his worst.

"I don't understand," Jeff was saying softly to himself, staring into the fire and shaking his head.

"Hmm?" Andy said.

"I don't understand," Jeff said again, louder this time. He looked up now – looked straight at Josh. "I don't understand."

"What?"

Jeff shook his head. "You're dead!" Standing, he wrung his hands in the air. "How can you die again? You're already dead!"

Josh nodded, understanding completely. Moving next to Jeff, he crouched near the fire.

"I know why you're frustrated," Josh said. "It doesn't make sense. None of it. Dead and still dying. The finished fight still being fought. It's crazy. When I first came here – when I died, I should say – I thought this was Hell. Only Hell could be so cruel as to offer battle to the battle-weary; flame to the burned; parched lips to the thirsty. I cursed God because He cursed me."

Throwing a rock angrily into the fire, Josh began to rant. "I was a Christian all my life. I went to church with my mama. I prayed every night before I went to bed because I didn't want Jesus to forget me if He decided to come back that night."

Standing, he raised his arms in the air and shouted, "This is my eternal reward! This is what I get for my faith and devotion! God has looked on me and spat in my face."

Falling to his knees, Josh sobbed, "I just want it to end. I can't take it no more."

He crouched there a moment, silent in his misery, rubbing his hands hard together as if trying to wipe away a filth that none of them could see.

For awhile, the only sound came from the slow popping of the fire; the crackle of oak in flames. When Josh finally looked up, he looked directly at Jeff.

"You needn't worry about the dead dying when they's already dead," he said. "We all die here. And every morning, soon as the sun comes up, everything's back the way it was. The cripples can walk again, the wounded are healed, and the dead are alive."

Jeff stared at him – stupefied. "No way! How can you keep dying?"

Josh shrugged. "I can't explain it. Wouldn't want to try. But I can tell you this, every time a bullet hits me, every time a shell knocks me to the ground or blows my leg or arm off, I feel it. The pain's just as real as it was the first time I was killed. And when you're wounded, ya just lie there and bleed, hurting and wanting to scream. It's just like that. Just like the first time."

Standing, he pulled his shirt high to expose his stomach and chest. "Look at me!" he hissed. "I've been killed over a thousand times and there ain't a scratch on me."

Dropping his shirt, he tapped the side of his head.

"It's the mind that's scarred. Damaged. The mind and the soul. Seems every time I die, every time I'm wounded, the pain makes me hate them damn Rebs all the more. I hated 'em when I died the first time, but I hate 'em more now. More than you can imagine."

Sitting, Josh whispered, "More than you can possibly imagine."

It was almost morning when the Marauders slipped quietly back into Gettysburg. The first birds of the morning were starting their chirping, warbling, and wailing. It was a sound that ushered in every Gettysburg morning, but on this morning Andy and the others felt as if they were hearing it for the first time.

It was a beautiful sound.

The sound of life.

God's music.

After clustering together for a few minutes behind the Civil War Emporium, with few words spoken between them, they separated and drifted off to their respective homes.

All were exhausted, but none would sleep.

Soft pillows would cushion their heads and womb-like blankets would surround them but sleep would evade their tired minds.

Too much had happened this night for them to sleep.

Sleep didn't matter.

The sun was rising in the east and the dead were rising from the mud on the southwest slope of Little Round Top. The soldiers they watched die the night before were standing now and brushing themselves off. There would be no sign of the previous night's slaughter.

No wounds.

No amputees.

No bodies.

The sun was up now.

And the dead walked the fields of Gettysburg.

28

Andy waited outside the Adams County Library a full twenty minutes before it finally opened at nine. After a quick "Hello" to Mrs. Bartholomew and April May, he disappeared behind one of the computerized card files and began searching for answers he wasn't likely to find.

After leafing through a dozen books on the occult, Eastern religions, life-after-death experiences, and angels, frustration was beginning to bear down on him. It wasn't the ghosts at Little Round Top he was concerned with. He had already accepted their presence because he could understand it – there was a reason they were there.

But Andy had seen more than ghosts at Little Round Top the previous night. He had seen evil stalking through the trees, stirring up tired men and pushing them back into battle with hate and vengeance on their minds. At first, he mistook this presence for a shadow, or a weird anomaly of the afterworld, floating around the men like a windswept fog – a black fog.

But it was more than this.

The presence seemed to drift to those men who had lost their will to fight – lost their will to hate. As tentacles of black mist wrapped around these men the fire would suddenly return to their eyes and with hatred seeping from every pore, they would plunge back into battle.

No one seemed to take any notice of the fog except Andy, as if they couldn't or wouldn't see it. But as the black mass drifted closer to him, Andy felt the hatred and loathing and knew the fog for what it was: an evil presence. A vile betrayer. Still nearer it drifted, stirring men from the stupor of battle and filling them with renewed hatred. Before he could shout a warning, the fog seemed to sense Andy's prying eyes and, like a startled rabbit, it bolted away from him, melting back into the trees.

Now, in a county library that had never heard of such things, Andy Martin searched for elusive answers. In the end, he was left to his own conclusions. Conclusions that told him the fog was indeed evil and that it was partly responsible for sustaining the hatred between the two armies for so long.

After two hours of research, Andy's only hope was found in a book about angels. There he found a telling passage: *Where evil goes, a redeeming spirit of light is sure to follow.* They were simple words, but they offered hope that somehow Josh and the others could be freed from their perpetual struggle. Reading the sentence again, Andy wondered how one goes about summoning a "spirit of light."

Shaking his head, he realized the absurdity of such a thought. You don't summon spirits; they work according to their own schedule, or to God's, but never according to the whims of man. Andy realized he would have to wait. This didn't bother him though, because he now knew that the spirit would eventually come. He was certain of it.

In time, the spirit of light would come.

29

Saturday, June 25
Back at Little Round Top

As the Marauders trudged up the rocky slope of Little Round Top for the second time in as many days, the ghostly tent slowly appeared out of the shadows before them. As it did, an icy finger ran up Andy's spine.

He found himself longing for the smell of gunpowder, the thrill of battle and the roar of musketry. He found himself desiring something that should not be desired and it alarmed him.

The night before he had watched men die.

Terrible deaths.

Lonely slaughter.

But – God forgive him – it was thrilling.

This was the ambrosia that had intoxicated men for as long as mankind had walked the planet. Alexander the Great, Caesar, Genghis Khan, Napoleon, and Hitler. All were men of battle and blood. All had come to feast at the table of War, sitting upon the bones of their dead.

Blood.

Battle.

Death.

War.

Andy knew that to eat such a bitter dish was sometimes a necessary evil. But to enjoy it!

That was an affront to God.

Following Josh silently into the tent, Andy paid more attention to the transformation this time. Hoping for a clue to the tent's magic. Once again, an incredible force jerked him off his feet and pulled him through the nebulous tunnel. Moving at what seemed to be a frightful speed, Andy extended his arms, as if flying. A moment later it was all over and he once again found himself standing inside the tent.

Exiting through the flap, Andy was surprised to see Jeff – who was still in the mortal world – walking toward him. Coming on as if he didn't see Andy, Jeff stepped toward the open flap and then, as Andy stood transfixed, Jeff walked *through* him.

Andy froze. "Did you see that?" he hissed at Matt.

Matt, whose mouth was hanging open, slowly nodded his head. "Too wicked! He went right through you – like you were a ghost."

A second later Jeff popped out of the tent.

Andy and Matt stared at him.

Checking himself quickly to see if something was missing, Jeff said, "What? What ya looking at?"

"You just walked through Andy," Matt explained.

At that moment Grant popped out of the tent.

"What do ya mean I walked through Andy?"

"When you were walking into the tent and Andy was coming out, you walked right through him."

Jeff was still confused. "I'm sorry, Andy. I didn't see you. You're not hurt, are you?"

"Never mind," Andy said. "It's nothing." But it wasn't; not to Andy. As Jeff passed through him their spirits touched, and for a moment they were as one. He felt Jeff's anxiety – his fear; as if they were two pieces of the same cosmic puzzle. It was like nothing he had experienced before in his life.

Hiking up the slope, Josh pointed to the road leading up from Devil's Den. "Can you see it?"

"What?" Andy said. "The road?"

"Yes. Can you see it?"

"Of course we can. Why wouldn't we?"

"I couldn't see it," Josh said. "Until recently, I could only see the world I died in. That road wasn't there when I died, so I couldn't see it. These monuments," he continued, pointing to the 44th New York's castle and the monument honoring the 16th Michigan, "I couldn't see them, either."

"Weird," Grant said. "Can the other ghosts see them?"

"No. Only I," Josh replied. "I think it is because of the tent; because I've crossed into your world. I don't know. It's hard to explain. Sometimes, during the day, I see people, many, many people walking around the camp. They wear strange clothing, like yours, and I can only assume they come from your world."

"And you couldn't see or hear any of this before?" Andy said. Josh shook his head.

"So, what's it mean?" Jeff asked.

Andy thought for a moment, pacing slowly around the group. "It could mean that somehow we're linked. You and us," he said, looking at Josh. "The mortal world and the immortal world." Glancing suspiciously toward the tent, he added, "I'm just wondering why the tent's there in the first place. It's like you were meant to cross over and if that's so, there's got to be a reason."

"Then we have to find the reason," Matt stated.

"Right. Only how do we do that?"

Josh was nodding his head. "Maybe you're right. And if so, we have to ask ourselves who put the tent there. After that, perhaps discovering a purpose will be a simpler proposition."

Grant had a quizzical look on his face. "Who? What do you mean, who?"

"He means," Andy said, "that the tent didn't just appear. Someone had to put it there for us to find – but who?"

Jeff seemed to brighten. "What about God?"

Andy nodded. "Maybe. Or it could have been an angel, a spirit of light," he said, betraying his thoughts.

"It could be more sinister than that," Josh said, looking apprehensively toward the tent. "We are forgetting that where you find angels, demons are not far behind."

Andy shook his head. "Why would demons allow us to cross over? I'd think they'd be afraid to let that happen. Remember, demons don't want people to know that there's a spirit, that's why they try to confuse us. Why would they weaken themselves by bringing us into the spirit world? I say they wouldn't. I say it wasn't demons that let us cross over, it was something else. If there's a good and evil in the universe, which I believe there is, this tent comes from the good side. I don't know how to explain

115

how I know this, I just do."

As Andy's words filtered through the sparse forest, a voice called to them from the north, "Josh? That you?"

Stiffening, Josh looked warily into the trees. "Who's there?"

There was a moment of silence. "It's me. Abraham," the voice finally called.

Josh exhaled a gasping sigh. "What are you doing sneaking around over there, Abe? You scared the ticks right off me."

"Them your friends?" Abe asked, stepping clear of the trees and stomping across the rocky terrain toward them.

"Yep. Come here and I'll make your acquaintance."

"Major Prichard is right 'hind me." Looking over his shoulder and seeing no Major, Abe scratched the side of his dirty face. "Leastwise, he was."

Just then a Union officer stepped from the trees, hands on his hips, studying the Marauders. "I'm here," Prichard said softly. He was only a major but his manner and words were presented with the icy confidence of a war-hardened general.

"These are the mortals." It was more of a statement then a question.

"Yessir," Josh snapped.

Walking with deliberately slow strides across the short distance that separated them, the major planted himself in front of the boys. "My name is Prichard, Major Jonathan Prichard." Turning, he stared down at Jeff. "Who might you be?"

"J-Jeff Kowalski, Sir."

Prichard kept his icy glare for a moment longer before his smile betrayed him. Reaching down, he placed Jeff's limp hand in his own and shook it. "A distinct pleasure to make your acquaintance."

As relief flooded Jeff's face, he looked for a moment like he might pass out. In the end, he steadied himself and it wasn't long before the color returned to his cheeks.

Turning to Matt, the major introduced himself again and shook hands. Then it was Grant's turn, and finally Andy's. Behind the major, Abraham followed, shaking hands and saying, "Scruggs, Abraham Scruggs. You can call me Abe."

In short order the group was chattering away like they had known one another for many years. Of particular interest to Andy

116

was the major's sword, an elaborate presentation model like none he had ever seen.

An armored knight with drawn sword adorned the top, forming the handle with his body. Above the knight was an eagle, perched and looking down. An ornate limb extended out from the eagle, then looped down and around to form the hilt. A number of scenes were also etched into the scabbard. A mother eagle with a flag draped around her three nesting eaglets; a pouncing lion with the sun rising above the clouds behind it. At the tip of the scabbard there was a winged angel, some stars, a globe and a skull and crossbones. As if this wasn't ornate enough, wrapped around the end of the scabbard was a cluster of acorns and leaves.

"It's rather strange," Major Prichard explained as he held out the sword for Andy's inspection. "When I died, I had my regulation sword with its bronze scabbard. I never presumed to carry my presentation sword into battle, for this would be to flirt with death."

"How did it wind up here, then?" Andy asked.

The major turned the corner of his mouth up and squinted his eyes. "I don't really know," he said, shaking his head shortly back and forth. "I know that I gave it to my wife to take back to New York on her last visit to Washington. When I awoke here" he said, holding his arms outstretched as if to encompass the battlefield, "it was by my side."

"Well, it's a wonderful sword," Andy said. "I've seen some originals before, but you can tell they're old and some are in really poor shape. Yours looks new. It's beautiful."

"I thank you for your generous words," Major Prichard said, bowing slightly to his new young friend.

A few feet away, Abe's voice broke above all others.

"No, honest. I'm seventeen years old. I joined up when I was fifteen – as a drummer, just like Josh."

"How come you're dressed like a regular soldier, then?" Matt pried.

"It's like this," Abe explained. "As the reg'ment started getting smaller and smaller, Colonel Chamberlain said I could take me a musket and be a regular soldier. I was a fisherman back in Maine. Didn't know what kind of soldier I'd make. But, I reckon the colonel didn't have much of a choice. 'Cause we lost so many men." Looking at Matt, then at Jeff, Abe said, "We fought a lot of battles. That we did." Pointing, as if to show them a picturesque scene, Abe said, "I was kilt right over there." He paused. "The first time, I mean. I been kilt a lot since then."

Raising his hands over his head, Major Prichard begged for their attention. "Boys! Listen to me a moment, please."

All fell silent.

"I need you to return through the tent. The Rebels will be attacking shortly and we can't take the chance of something happening to you."

"We were all right last night," Andy argued.

The major smiled. "Frankly, that was a piece of foolhardy work last night. We have no idea what would happen to you in your own world if you were to die here. It's a thing we cannot afford to find out. I am the senior Union officer here and I tell you that you are welcome anytime . . . but not during battle. I won't take that risk."

Grant screwed up his face tight. "Does this mean we gotta go? I mean, we just got here."

Prichard's eyes were apologetic. "I'm afraid it's necessary."

"We'll take the risk! I'll take the risk!" Andy stated.

"No."

There was silence.

A hesitation.

Finally, Matt was the one to break the standoff. "He's right, Andy. We don't know what'll happen to us if we get hurt or killed. Besides, we probably shouldn't be here anyway when they're fighting. I have this feeling that it's wrong. You know?"

Andy bowed his head. He hated to admit it but he knew Matt was right. "Okay. You win."

Walking back down to the tent, it took another ten minutes to say their good-byes. Finally, one by one, the Marauders disappeared through the flap.

Andy was the last to go.

Turning as he entered, he smiled back at the three ghosts who had befriended them. "You promise we can come back?"

"You have my word," Major Prichard replied.

Looking at Josh, Andy said, "I'll bring my drum next time. Remember, you promised to teach me how to play."

"I remember."

As Andy let the flap close behind him, a Confederate cannon boomed in the distance, followed quickly by another, and then another. A moment later the air throbbed as Union artillery on the crest above opened up in defiant response.

The battle was on.

30

Monday, June 27

It was just before eleven when the mailman came to the Martin house, lugging his bulging sack and perspiring slightly in the June heat. Lifting the lid on the Martin mailbox, he stuffed it with a bill, two coupon fliers, a sweepstakes entry form, and a letter from the National Archives at Eighth Street and Pennsylvania Avenue in Washington, D.C.

It was addressed to Andy.

"Morning, Larry," Alice said with a smile and a wave as she pushed open the screen door.

Larry, already at the end of the walkway, looked over his shoulder and shot her a wide grin. "Morning," he said, waving back.

He didn't stop to chat, though.

Larry was in a hurry. He was always in a hurry. For three years he had maintained the fastest delivery rate in all of Adams county, a record he was proud of. Funny thing was that because he was so fast, his route kept growing and growing. A house here, a street there. The faster Larry worked, the more his route grew. He never complained, though. Not Larry. He had worked for the government long enough to know how the system worked. Reward the efficient with more work until they reach the point of inefficiency.

119

That was the government.

Larry didn't really mind the extra work. He liked being a mailman. He liked the people. He liked the outdoors. And yes, he even liked the snow.

Larry was the last of a dying breed.

Shuffling through the mail, Alice spied the letter from the National Archives and studied it curiously. "Andy!" she called from the entry.

"Yeah? I'm in my room."

"Honey, you got a letter from the National Archives. Did you order something?"

The clank, thump, and clamor from upstairs told Alice that the letter was indeed expected. A moment later Andy darted into the hall and raced down the stairs, taking them two at a time.

"What is it? Let me see!"

Alice held the letter out to him, then mischievously snatched it back as he reached for it.

"Mom!"

"All right," Alice smiled, handing him the letter. Taking the government envelope by the corner, Andy quickly broke the gummed seal with his thumb and extract three official-looking forms.

"What in the world are you up to?" Alice asked with that quirky smile she always put on when she thought Andy was being cute.

Andy shrugged as he quickly scanned the forms. "Just doing some research," he said absently.

"Research? Good grief! You just finished the school year."

"It's not school work. Just something I'm working on."

Trying to read over Andy's shoulder but failing, Alice just shook her head. "Your father gets that way, too. Just like that. All quiet and contemplative. I swear you two are like peas in a pod sometimes."

Turning without further inquisition, Alice went back to the living room; back to her needlepoint.

"National Cemetery," Andy whispered to himself, tapping the paper with an idle finger. But the spark in his eye was enough to set any decent mother to fretting.

Stuffing the envelope in his pocket, he yelled, "I'm going out, Mom. See ya." And then the screen door banged and he was gone.

31

National Cemetery was dedicated on Thursday, November 19, 1863. Originally conceived as a resting place for those men who died in the terrible fighting around Gettysburg, the cemetery now offered rest to the dead soldiers of other American wars as well.

It was at the dedication of National Cemetery that one of the most memorable speeches in American history was presented. And though this speech was short, lasting only a few minutes, Lincoln's Gettysburg Address was interrupted five times by the enthusiastic applause of over fifteen thousand men, women, and children. Spectators who had gathered for the dedication. When Lincoln finished, there was hearty applause, followed by three cheers for the president and the governors of the states.

The ceremony actually began at ten o'clock that morning with a procession through the main streets of Gettysburg. A heavy fog lingered over the town as the procession made its way to the cemetery. At eleven fifteen, after the performance of a funeral dirge, the Reverend Stockton delivered a stirring prayer. As his words floated over the heads of the crowd, the fog suddenly broke and radiant sunlight poured upon the gathered masses.

God's grace, some would say.

The rest of the day was filled with speeches, both great and small. Governors from a number of states were present and some took their turn at the podium. It is said that the crowd was so silent that every word uttered was clearly heard by all fifteen thousand present.

At six o'clock that evening, President Lincoln boarded his train for the return trip to Washington. As he left the little town of Gettysburg behind, reporters were already relaying the text of his speech to newspapers around the Union. City by city, county by county, state by state, men and women would read his immortal words and their hearts would be stirred.

They would remember.

One short speech, written for the dedication of a simple soldier's cemetery, would endure for generations to come.

In 1776, a nation of destiny was born of cannon fire and musket shot upon a new continent. Our Founding Fathers helped define the character of this new nation and endeavored to teach it right from wrong. It was through their moral courage that the United States was able to take a stand on the side of freedom and democracy.

The nation grew.

With every pen stroke of the Constitution, with every right, and with every self-evident truth, the nation continued to grow. But it wasn't until November 19, 1863, that the nation reached maturity.

Thanks to the words of a teacher named Lincoln.

* * *

The muffled drum's sad roll has beat
the soldier's last tattoo,
No more on life's parade shall meet
the brave and fallen few.

On fame's eternal camping-ground,
their silent tents are spread,
And glory guards with solemn round,
the bivouac of the dead.

The Bivouac of the Dead
— Theodore O'Hara

Riding down Breckenridge, then taking a right on South Washington Street, Andy and Matt rode side by side. Their pedals whirling their whisper-quiet song.

"I hate cemeteries," Matt muttered as they paused for the light at the busy intersection at Steinwehr Avenue. "How do you know he's buried there?"

"I got a letter from the National Archives in Washington. I should have thought to check at the cemetery first, I guess. It just never occurred to me."

122

The light turned green and they crossed over to Taneytown Road. Stopping in front of the National Park Service Visitor Center at the top of the hill, they waited for traffic to pass.

"How come he was buried here?" Matt asked as they waited.

"A lot of Union soldiers were buried here after the battle. I did a paper on it last year for Mr. Varga's history class."

As the last car passed, the boys crossed the street and entered Gettysburg National Cemetery.

"Right after the battle, most of the dead were buried in shallow graves right where they died," Andy explained. "Even the Confederates. But by the end of July some of the graves were starting to wash out. It rained a lot that month and I guess the bodies weren't buried deep enough. Or maybe it was because the ground had been dug up and disturbed, I don't know. But the bodies were starting to stick up and people realized they had to do something. The other problem was that the markers they used to identify the dead were just old boards that they had carved the names into. It didn't take long for them to start to fade."

"How come they didn't send the bodies home so their families could bury them?"

"Some were sent home. But they had already been in the ground and it was a messy business to dig them up and move them. After awhile, the guys who were exhuming the bodies and escorting them to their families started to complain. Someone must have decided that there had to be a better way to bury them properly. That's why National Cemetery was proposed."

"So after they made the cemetery, they moved all the bodies here?"

"Yeah."

"How many?"

"It was over thirty-five hundred. A lot of them are unidentified, though. They just know that they're Union. There's like two or three sections just for the unknowns. I guess it was a little difficult at first, separating the Union from the Confederate."

"Why?"

"Because the Confederates had a hard time getting uniforms and sometimes they wore confiscated Union clothing. The only way they could tell if the body was Confederate for certain was by the underwear."

"They had underwear back then?"

"Well, it was kind of like underwear. They didn't have Fruit of the Loom or anything like that. But they had cotton underclothing and whenever Weaver – he was the guy responsible for moving the bodies – whenever he saw cotton underclothes he knew it was a Rebel."

"What about the others? The ones who are known?"

"They're buried according to State. Originally, they were going to be buried randomly, but one of the states protested; Massachusetts, I think. Yeah, that's right. Anyway, it was decided that each state should get its own plot."

"So Josh is buried in the Pennsylvania plot."

"Yeah. The plots are arranged in a semicircle and all the bodies were buried with the head pointing toward the center of the half-circle. That's where the Soldier's National Monument now stands. Which is nice, if you think about it. Anyway, the Pennsylvania plot is in the outer circle, almost halfway around the arch."

Arriving at the first row of dead, all unknowns, Andy pointed to the north.

"Josh should be over there. Row B."

Making their way past the small rectangular markers of the unknowns, they soon found themselves looking at the markers for Indiana. Then Ohio, Massachusetts, and finally Pennsylvania.

The markers were stark and informal.

Name and unit was all that was provided.

Stumbling down row B, Andy quickly found the stone marker.

"Joshua Harding," he read. "Eighty-Third PA."

They sat on the grass next to the marker for several minutes before speaking. It was strange to think that Josh's body was lying three feet below them. Strange because Josh was their friend and it's hard to think of your friends as being dead – especially when you still talk to them on a regular basis.

"We should have brought some flowers," Matt said, picking absently at a blade of grass. "We always brought flowers when we visited my mom."

"We can bring some tomorrow," Andy offered.

124

Matt nodded, then felt guilty because at that moment he was no longer thinking about Josh, but about another grave two thousand miles away. A grave that deserved flowers, but had none.

Sure, Matt thought. *Tomorrow we'll bring flowers.*

32

At four-thirty that morning, Josh appeared in the corner of Andy's room. He didn't wake his mortal friend immediately, but stood silently and watched him inhale and exhale in his slumber. Slow breaths, drawn quietly from clean Pennsylvania air, filling the lungs with life and energy.

For ten full minutes Joshua watched in thoughtful silence. Then, quietly, he said, "Andy!"

Andy's rhythmic breathing faltered for a moment as he grumbled in his sleep and turned on his side.

"Andy!" Josh said again, louder this time.

Sitting up, Andy looked around the room.

"It's me, Andy," Josh said, stepping from the corner.

Wiping the sleep from his eyes, Andy said, "Josh? What's wrong?"

"Nothing."

Andy yawned. "What time is it?"

"Late. I'm sorry to wake you but I thought I must see you. To thank you."

"For what?"

"I saw you and Matt today. At the cemetery."

"Ah, that was nothing," Andy said.

Shaking his head, Josh said, "No, it is something of great importance to me. You have honored me and I won't soon forget it."

"I just thought we should know where you're buried," Andy explained. "I mean, you're our friend. I just thought it was the decent thing to do."

125

Smiling, Josh said, "It was the most decent thing any soul has done for me since I died. Now go back to sleep. I did not mean to disturb your rest. I just wanted to thank you." Stepping back into the shadows, he said, "I won't forget."

Then he was gone.

"Geez," Andy complained to the empty room as a shiver tickled his spine. "I wish you wouldn't do that, Josh. Ya give me the heebie-jeebies."

But Andy was soon fast asleep, breathing deeply once again. He was getting used to dealing with ghosts and their haunting ways.

Besides, the heebie-jeebies never last long.

33

Monday, July 4

At ten o'clock sharp the fireworks began lighting up the sky over Gettysburg, bursting into kaleidoscopic displays that trickled slowly back down to earth in splendor and glory. Sitting on their bikes outside of town and wearing backpacks that were full to bursting, the Marauders watched the blooms and listened to the reports with the usual awe and excitement associated with fireworks.

After all, they were boys and these were explosives.

The two went together like Bonnie and Clyde.

Like fire and cracker.

As always, Gettysburg promised a full half hour of explosive excitement for the tourists who gathered for the annual reenactment. And, as always, Gettysburg delivered. The spectacular display drew to a close in a crescendo of bursts and reports that grew momentously and then ended abruptly. Cascading echoes of manmade thunder lingered in the night sky for a precarious moment, then scattered like bats before a new dawn.

Silence followed; as if the town paused for a theatrical breath and a much deserved bow. The glow of a spent rocket as it tumbled slowly back to earth begged for applause.

Jeff watched what was left of the ember shrouded rocket as it fell from the sky and disappeared into a nearby field. "That was way better than last year!"

Grant nodded enthusiastically. "Yeah, too cool! It reminds me of when my cousin worked in the fireworks factory and they had this four-alarm fire from someone smoking in the bathroom. The whole place went up. Ka-bloo-ee! Blasted a crater in the ground a hundred feet deep and he said the fireworks were going off over the town for a week."

Andy, Matt, and Jeff rolled their eyes in unison.

"It's true!" Grant said. "Honest!"

"Come on," Andy said, "we've got a show of our own to do."

"I'm telling you, it's true!" Grant insisted as they turned their bikes to the south.

"Yeah," Matt said, "like the time the meteor hit your uncle's car and slammed it twenty feet into the ground."

Grant's finger was wagging now as he lectured. "That's true! I swear! You can call my cousin, Pete. He'll tell you. It was a Cadillac Seville and the meteor slammed it twenty feet into the ground. They had to get a bulldozer to dig it out. It was all munched and it had this meteor stuff on it."

Matt was shaking his head. "Got any pictures to prove it?"

"My camera broke."

Once again, eyes rolled.

"No really. It worked fine until the meteor hit. Then – ppplltt – nothing. Nada. Zilch."

"Get the meteor and maybe we'll believe you," Andy said.

Grant thought about this for a moment, then smiled. "I will. Just watch, I'll call my cousin Pete. Then you'll see."

"I can hardly wait," Matt smirked.

A brisk, ten-minute ride carried them to the parking lot atop Little Round Top. Dropping their bikes in the woods fifty feet from the road, they quickly made their way to the tent.

Josh was waiting.

He watched with amusement as the Marauders huffed and

puffed their way up the trail. "Where's your surprise?" he asked as they drew near.

"You'll . . . see," Andy panted.

Giving them a few minutes to catch their breath, Josh led the way through the tent and then up to the crest of Little Round Top, to the Union camp. Tents were pitched here and there, with campfires crackling a sleepy song of embers as the men milled about. Some cleaned weapons, while others talked softly among themselves. Some stared quietly into the fire as their minds wandered through dark places only they could go, mesmerized by the flame, as if it were their personal demon come to haunt them.

"We'll set up on that flat rock near the ridge," Andy said, pointing to a spot a dozen yards from the nearest tent.

Jeff suddenly slapped the heel of his hand into his forehead. "Did anyone bring matches?"

"Relax," Matt said, "I got 'em. A couple punks, too. That way we don't have to burn up all our matches right away."

"Should we let them know we're gonna start?" Grant asked. "Or just go ahead and start lighting?"

Andy nodded toward the tents, "We better let them know. Otherwise they'll think the Confederates are attacking. Who wants to go?"

"I'll do it," Josh said. Without waiting, he shot off toward the tent city that was the Union camp. Soon, an excited commotion arose inside Prichard's tent and quickly spread to the men clustered around the nearby fires. Throwing the flap aside, Josh dashed from Prichard's tent and disappeared among the maze of men and fires. A minute later the eager blare of a bugle called the brigade to muster.

Standing before his men, Major Prichard had a game sparkle in his eyes. With the skill of a Shakespearean actor, he waited silently before his men just long enough to build drama. Then he spoke. "Our friends from the other world have prepared a special treat for us tonight. I don't know what they have in store for us, but I am eager to lend them my attention. I urge you to do the same."

Finishing, Prichard turned to Matt and Andy and signaled for them to begin. As all eyes in the camp turned to the young

Marauders, Jeff and Grant hastily scurried away, leaving Matt and Andy to face the brigade of ghosts.

Feeling his palms clam up, Andy rubbed his hands together. "Since you all have been so nice to us, we thought we'd bring some fireworks for you," Andy said. "After all, today's the Fourth of July."

A murmur ran through the group. Most of them stopped keeping track of the days over a century before. Days didn't matter in the afterworld. Years mattered even less. But now, hearing that it was the Fourth – Independence Day – many of the men couldn't help smiling. It was like waking up one summer morning only to discover that it was actually Christmas and the most magnificent tree one could imagine was in the living room with presents piled high around it.

It was the most pleasant of surprises.

As Andy and Matt quickly unloaded the fireworks from their backpacks, separating the fountains from the rockets, the men of Little Round Top fell easily into the holiday spirit. Clapping one another on the back they began to sing. Soon, the hillside rang with Union merriment as the wary Confederates at Devil's Den ventured from their positions to see what mischief was afoot.

With both hands, Matt hoisted up a missile battery appropriately named the SCREAM'N DEMON. "What about this one first?"

Andy grinned widely and nodded. "Do it!" Passing a lit punk to Matt, he stepped clear of the fire zone.

Silence descended upon the hill as the fuse sparked and the flame began to race toward its singular destiny. With a spectacular roar the twenty-round battery cut loose, lighting the sky with blooming flowers of red, white, and blue. Each bloom erupted with a loud report that rolled down the slope of Little Round Top and echoed boisterously off the craggy formations at Devil's Den.

"Oooo!" the camp sang. "Awwww!"

Taking turns, Andy and Matt sent one rocket after another into the waiting sky. Those Confederates not already watching this aerial display were now drawn from their fires and tents. Congregating on top of the highest peaks at Devil's Den, their eyes rose to the sky.

It wasn't long before the two armies found themselves cheering the bursts in unison, clapping and hooting with growing enthusiasm from their respective positions. They watched the aerial display with the fascination of children who find themselves longing for simpler times and simpler passions. The Blue and the Gray faced each other across the Valley of Death that night; enemies united in a common purpose.

Josh later commented that it was the first night since the summer of '63 that a battle had not been fought. Which goes to prove that giving explosives to pre-teen boys isn't necessarily a bad thing.

Sometimes it makes a miracle.

34

Saturday, July 9

In all the decades that battle had raged on the hills and fields of Gettysburg, no flag of truce had ever been advanced to the enemy camp. No quarter was asked for by the spectral warriors of Gettysburg . . . and none was given.

Until now.

After two nights of bitter fighting, the Confederates were once again in control of Devil's Den. The previous night had seen bold action as the Confederate commander, Colonel Harlow, pressed hard against the Union left flank. Unrelenting in his determination to retake his beloved rocks, the Rebel commander urged his men into battle from the stained saddle of a hell-black mare. With saber glistening in the eerie glow of the afterworld, the colonel charged the enemy position – then fell dead as a dozen musket balls tore him apart. Enraged, the colonel's men slammed into the Union line, forcing a hasty retreat back up the rocky slope of Little Round Top. Tonight, eager to regain the lost ground, Major Prichard launched a bloody campaign to throw the Rebels back.

But now came the flag.

With a tattered white cloth tied loosely to the barrel of a Colt Model 1855 rifle, two Confederates advanced toward the Union position. The maddening *crack-crack-crack* of musketry and the drone of artillery faltered, then died completely as both sides paused in disbelief.

When the exchange of fire stopped, Major Prichard stepped from behind a sizeable boulder and advanced to meet the Rebels. Words were exchanged at a dozen paces and Andy saw the Confederates point in his direction.

"What's going on?" Jeff asked. "Is it a surrender?"

"A sergeant and a private?" Andy said. "Not likely. If it was a surrender, their senior officers would have to initiate it."

"Then what are they doing?"

Andy shrugged.

Turning, Major Prichard picked his way back up the slope of Little Round Top while the Confederates waited behind. The look on his face told of his displeasure. When he was halfway up the hill, Prichard waved the boys down.

Andy pointed at himself and the major nodded. "Looks like we're being summoned," he said. Standing and glancing up the slope to the crest of Little Round Top, Andy searched for Josh, but there was no sign of him. Resignedly, he turned and led the way down the hill.

"What's he want us for?" Jeff asked, stumbling along behind.

"Maybe they want to trade us for prisoners or something," Grant offered. "When my Grandpap was in France with the underground, they traded some German prisoners for one of their underground leaders. Bet that's what they're doing."

Matt snorted and shook his head but said nothing.

"We're not prisoners," Andy reminded Grant.

"So?"

"So! They're not going to trade us! Besides, Major Prichard is our friend."

"Maybe Grant's right," Jeff said, a confused look on his face. "Who knows how these ghosts do things. This might be a trick to steal our bodies so they can live again."

Stopping, Andy turned and looked first at Jeff, then at Grant. "You two been eating stupid-pills or something? That's the dumbest thing I ever heard. Josh is our friend. Major Prichard is our friend. The whole Union Army is our friend. This isn't major league baseball, Queens of Dork. They're not going to trade us to the other team. Now shut up and let's go. We're holding up the war."

Without waiting for a response, Andy turned and continued down the slope, muttering words none could hear and shaking his head in disbelief.

"Your presence has been requested," Major Prichard called as Andy, Matt, Jeff, and Grant approached.

Matt pointed to the Confederates. "By them?"

"Yes, I'm afraid so," Major Prichard replied. "They would not tell me the nature of their business, but apparently they felt it urgent enough to risk being shot. This is exactly why I didn't want you here during battle. Poor timing on our part, I'm afraid. But then, there's little we can do about it now. Will you speak with them?"

"Sure," Andy said, looking to the others for unanimity.

"Why not?" Matt grinned.

"They're not going to shoot us are they?" Grant said, but only Jeff heard.

When they were a dozen paces from the bedraggled Confederates, Major Prichard held his hand up for them to stop. "These are the boys you asked to speak with. I suggest you state your business quickly and keep a civil tongue or you'll have no more of our patience."

The Rebel sergeant was the first to speak. He was a silver-bearded man with a thinning crown; probably in his early fifties. By the look of him, Andy guessed he was a farmer before the war.

"They says you boys is from the living world. That right?" The sergeant's voice was rough; like he'd been gargling gravel and forgot to spit when he finished.

"We're not dead, if that's what you mean," Andy replied.

The old Rebel nodded. "It's like this, boys. We was kilt over'n a nearby field. Me and George here," he pointed to the private next to him, "and three others from our brigade. Only we wasn't prop'ly buried. The damn–" he hesitated, eyeing Major Prichard. "The Yanks buried the five of us in a common grave an' forgat us. We been buried there ev'r since. It just ain't proper. Our kin not

132

knowin' where we're restin' and all. See what I mean?"

"Your bodies are still buried in the field?" Andy said. "You're sure?" As he spoke, a shiver started at the lower end of Andy's tailbone and ran its icy finger all the way up to the base of his skull. For the briefest moment he wondered if it was a shiver of morbid curiosity or just plain excitement.

"I ain't never known a spirit that didn't know where his body were," the old sergeant replied. "We was hopin' you'd see we get buried proper, with a marker an' all."

Andy nodded. "Of course."

The Confederates exchanged a look of surprise. "You mean you'll do it?"

"Of course."

The hard, tight lips of the Confederate sergeant now gave way to a warm smile. "We're much in yer debt."

"Can you show us where you're buried?" Andy asked.

Glancing from Andy to Prichard, the sergeant said, "Reckon so, if'n it's all right with the major."

Prichard hesitated, then nodded his approval. "We can't go with you, though," he told Andy. Then, scowling at the sergeant, "I have your word as a gentleman that they'll not be harmed or detained in any way?"

"My word," the sergeant promised, holding his right hand rigidly in the air as if to swear on a bible.

"For what that's worth," Prichard muttered under his breath. Waving the boys on, he said, "Do what you must."

Before starting back up the hill, however, the major shot Andy a look of concern; a contorted grimace that urged caution above all else. *Never trust a Reb,* he often told his men. And here he was ignoring his own advice.

To make matters worse, the major knew how quickly the whims of youth could turn to carelessness. Prudence, he realized, is a hard trait to impose on eager young minds. Frankly, it's a concept most boys won't fully grasp for another ten or fifteen years – for some, even longer.

After a considerable amount of coaxing, Andy led the Confederates reluctantly up Little Round Top and – after more coaxing – into the ghost tent. Tonight's work would be best conducted on the mortal side of existence. Corpses belong to the temporal.

35

The Wheatfield

On the late afternoon of July 2, 1863, a bloody game was played out on a field of trampled grain south of Gettysburg. Known after that simply as The Wheatfield, it proved to be one of the most contested fields of the battle.

Moving in from the south and west, Confederate troops under General McLaws and General Hood threw themselves at the weak Union line. A line stretching from Little Round Top all the way to the Peach Orchard by Emmitsburg Road. Like a turkey sticking its neck out on Thanksgiving, the Blue soldiers overextended themselves and now they would pay the price for such folly.

Union troops of Caldwell's Second Corps fought the Rebel onslaught in a fierce struggle that raged back and forth across The Wheatfield six times.

A summer storm of lead and steel.

A whirlwind of slaughter.

In fighting that was brutal and often hand to hand, Confederate forces finally managed to crush the Union line. The bold and foolhardy Union advance by General Sickles' Third Corps earlier that day now gave way to disaster. Falling back to Plum Run and Little Round Top, the Union retreat soon disintegrated into a complete rout.

In the aftermath of the bloody battle, thousands of men lay dead and dying in the much contested Wheatfield. Among them, Sergeant Benjamin Moser, one of General Anderson's hard fighting Georgians.

36

"Here it is, under this here tree," the old Confederate sergeant said, halting next to an ancient hickory. The trunk of the tree had a wide girth that was deeply furrowed, like the wrinkled skin of an ancient wood sprite. The bark appeared shaggy, something not uncommon to older hickory trees. In places, weathered scars could still be seen where both minie ́ ball and artillery had damaged the trunk. From the depth of these scars it was surprising the tree had survived.

Perhaps the blood-soaked soil of The Wheatfield had nourished it back to life. Or, perhaps a better explanation was that the roots of the old hickory now gnawed on the bones of five Confederate dead.

Ample nourishment for any tree.

"You're sure this is the tree?" Andy asked.

"That's it," Private George McCoy said, patting the tree almost affectionately. "Jus' like Benjamin said. We's buried on the north side, right under my foot here." George stomped the ground several times, as if trying to wake his corpse from its slumber.

"We'll have to get shovels," Matt suggested.

"We're not really going to dig them up ourselves, are we?" Jeff said, a look of horror on his face.

"Yes, we are," Andy replied.

"Why can't we just tell the Rangers, let them do it?"

"What are we going to tell them?" Andy asked. "That a couple of Confederate ghosts told us they were still buried in The Wheatfield and would we please dig them up?"

Jeff hesitated, opened his mouth, then closed it and chose silence over his fear.

"Why can't we leave the Rangers a note?" Grant interjected.

"They'd think it was a hoax," Matt said. "Andy's right, we've got to do this ourselves."

Andy was pacing slowly back and forth in front of the tree now, his right thumb and index finger caressing his chin. "I think

I've got an idea," he said. Reaching into his shirt pocket, he pulled out a ballpoint pen. "Anyone got a piece of paper?"

Grant, Jeff, and Matt started fishing in their pockets but all came up empty.

"I need something to write on," Andy said. "Anything."

"There's a garbage can over by the road," Jeff said. "It might have an old wrapper or something."

"Great idea," Andy said, visibly pleased.

Surprised that he had come up with a winning idea, Jeff beamed as Andy patted him on the shoulders and said, "Hop over there and see what you can find."

Jeff was so pleased with himself that he was halfway to the garbage can before he realized what he had gotten himself into. "Oh, man!" he muttered.

Sifting through the garbage can, grumbling and complaining at the stench and filth, Jeff spilled the can's contents onto the ground with little regard for the mess he was causing. With half the can now laying at his feet, he dropped to his knees and started picking through the rubbish.

"This is disgusting," he yelled.

Looking over at the tree, he was disappointed to find that no one was paying any attention to him. "Gross," he mumbled, pushing a soiled diaper away with a stick.

Spying a crumpled white paper bag under a half-eaten hamburger, Jeff reached out and picked it up gently, getting ketchup on his palm despite his caution. Wiping his hand on the ground next to him, he tried to smooth out the bag.

"I've got something," he said, waving the bag in the air as he stood and started back to the tree.

No one heard.

"I've got something," he repeated when he was a few yards away.

Standing, Andy nodded. "That'll work fine." Taking the bag, he crouched back down and rested it on his knee with pen at the ready. "Okay, Ben," he said, looking into the old sergeant's eyes, "give me the names again."

37

By one o'clock that morning the mist had returned. Creeping to the edge of Gettysburg, it stopped; as if entrance to the sleeping town was forbidden.

A white blanket lay silently over the low fields, a sea of foam searching for a shore to crash upon but finding only disappointment. It was a sea unfit for ship or raft. Unfit for a large pirate galleon bristling with guns and flying the grinning skull and crossbones over a rolling deck.

The mist was unfit for these things, and no brave pirate dared sail such a sea.

But the Marauders still came.

Pirates on bikes.

Treasure hunters.

On lifeless horses of steel they raced through the dewy mist, leaving a swirling wake behind them to mark their passage. Tonight the Marauders chased not gold, but the bones of the dead. Their Treasure Island lay in the field of a long-spent battle and their Long John Silver wore Confederate gray.

Tonight would be an adventure.

* * *

Turning off Steinwehr Avenue onto Queen Street, the Marauders pedaled toward the Kowalski residence five blocks away. They passed Grant's house on the left, sitting silent and in shadows. The porch light was off and all was in slumber. The neighborhood was quiet and serene; unaware that pirates roamed the streets.

Pulling off the road in front of Jeff's house, the Marauders cringed as their tires crunched loudly on the gravel at the shoulder.

Pop pop pop.

It sounded like so many firecrackers snapping inside a steel drum. The night's shrouded silence made it seem that much louder. Two houses up, a collie named Penny stood and barked, her keen ears rousing her quickly from a watchful slumber.

She sniffed the air.

Barked.

Then sniffed again.

Just the pirates, she realized after a third sniff. She thought it was a prowler — hoped it was a prowler — but it wasn't. There was never any excitement on Long Lane. No prowlers. No cats. No excitement.

Just those pirates.

The low grumble deep in Penny's throat died out before reaching the maturity of a full-grown bark. Quietly, she lay back down to sleep, her head resting nicely on her paws.

Penny was disappointed.

"You know where your dad keep it?" Andy whispered to Jeff, intentionally dropping the *S*-sound on 'keeps'. Like the shadow warriors they often imitated, the Marauders knew that the hiss of a spoken *S* carries far and can betray a whispered conversation.

"It in the 'ed," Jeff whispered, carefully observing the S-rule. "That where he keep it. I hope he didn't lock the door."

"We'll wait here," Matt said.

Jeff nodded apprehensively.

Unlatching the back gate, he pulled it to . . . slowly . . . gently. Taking his time so that the complaints of the rusting hinges wouldn't be so loud. *Got to oil this stupid gate,* Jeff thought, biting his lower lip and casting a wary eye up at his parent's window.

Through the gate he made a beeline for the shed, treading cautiously for fear of tripping over one of his little sister's toys. The backyard was black as shipbuilder's pitch. Even the scant bit of starlight they had enjoyed on the road was gone, snuffed out by the large oak that graciously held Fort Apache in its outstretched arms. Fumbling around in the dark, Jeff found the door latch and the MasterCraft padlock that usually hung open.

It was snapped shut.

Muttering an innocent vulgarity, Jeff stepped to the side of the shed and dropped to his knees. Searching the ground for the key he knew his father kept hidden, he was forced to rely on his hands because his eyes were all but useless in the thick darkness. In frustration, he soon gave up.

"It locked," Jeff hissed as he appeared out of the darkness in front of the Marauders.

"Great! What now?" Grant whined.

138

"Where the key?" Andy asked.

"One in the hou'," Jeff whispered, pointing to the front door. "But my dad keep a 'pare in one of tho' rock."

"What?"

"You know, tho' fake rock that are hollow? You put them in your flower bed to hide a key."

Andy was nodding his head. "Where the rock?"

"I couldn't find it."

"Did your dad move it?"

"I don't think 'o," Jeff shrugged.

"Well, than it got to be there."

"Take the light," Matt offered.

"That ju't what I wa' thinking," Andy said. Swinging his knapsack off his shoulder, he quickly unzipped it. A second later the hooded flashlight was in his hand. "Okay, let go."

At the shed, Andy discovered that the rock was exactly where it should have been; Jeff was just looking in the wrong place. Picking up the fake stone and popping open the back, Andy effortlessly unlocked the MasterCraft and eased the shed door open.

"There," Jeff said, pointing.

Hanging neatly from a wall hanger was a shovel with a manufacturer's label still glued to its shiny blade. Taking it by the wooden handle, Jeff also grabbed the spade hanging next to the door. The shovel was fine for bulk work, but when they were close to the bodies more delicate work would be required.

Wouldn't want to break a rib.

Benjamin might not like that.

Locking the shed and replanting the key, Andy and Jeff slipped back through the gate and out to the road.

"Who gonna carry the 'hovel?" Jeff asked, a subtle hint that he had no intention of carrying it all the way back to The Wheatfield.

"I'll take it," Matt said.

"We're ready then, huh?" Grant mused.

They all grumbled a "Yeah" and an "Uh-huh" but the silence that followed told more than their words would betray.

They were scared.

"We'd better get going," Andy said after sitting for too long and thinking too many thoughts.

No one answered.

They just mounted their bikes and started down the road, knowing full well where that road was leading them. Knowing that the mist hid more than the dark shadows of a dark night.

Out in a field under an old hickory tree, the bones of five dead soldiers waited to drink sunlight again.

And morning was only a breath away.

38

Sunday, July 10

It was shortly after nine when Clair Ames boomed into the Civil War Emporium. She *boomed* not because she was necessarily a boisterous person, but because she was ripe with excitement.

And Clair wasn't the type of woman who excited easily.

She had seen and heard enough — experienced enough — in her fifty-two years to encourage a more reserved and contemplative outlook on life. The sudden death of her husband in 1991 taught her a powerful lesson about loss. Grief almost destroyed her. But Clair wasn't one to give up on life so easily. A year after Morgan's death, she purchased the ten-room bed and breakfast next to the Emporium and fell easily into the role of businesswoman. Clair enjoyed her success with reserved passion – with dignified pride. Above all, she was a confident woman. It was this that first attracted Ed.

"Did you hear?" she asked as she hurried over to the counter.

"Hear what?"

"Oh, my! Out at The Wheatfield! You haven't heard yet?"

"I haven't heard anything," Ed said, half his attention devoted to Clair, the other half distracted by a rusted canteen he had purchased earlier that morning. "What am I supposed to have heard?"

"Why, someone dug up some old soldiers last night, on the battlefield."

"You're kidding!"

"No, honest. I heard it from one of the Rangers who found the note."

"What note?"

"The note that was taped to the front door of the Cyclorama this morning when they opened up. It said there were five Confederate soldiers buried at The Wheatfield, simple as that. Sure enough, when the Rangers got to The Wheatfield they found a hole under some old tree where someone was digging and there were these bones popping up." She shivered. "Like to give me goose bumps just thinking of it. They're out there now, the Rangers and some of the county police, sealing the area off, and I heard that they're calling in some archeologists to dig up the bodies. Anyway, the whole town is a-buzz."

Picking up the phone from the stand behind the counter, Ed quickly dialed a number and waited for the ring.

"Who ya calling?" Clair asked with curious eyes.

"Warren Feldman."

"Isn't he that Ranger friend of yours?"

"Sort of. He's the operations manager for the Park."

After two rings, Ed heard someone pick up.

"Gettysburg National Military Park, may I help you?" a woman's voice whispered in Ed's ear.

"Warren Feldman, please."

"I'm sorry. Mr. Feldman is out of the office and I don't expect him back for some time."

"Susie? Is that you?"

"Yes," came the hesitant reply.

"This is Ed. Ed Williams."

"Why, Edward, I didn't recognize that sweet voice of yours. Maybe if you'd call more often you wouldn't catch me by surprise like that."

Ed chuckled. "Sorry, Susie. Warren told me to quit hitting on his Rangers. What's a guy to do?"

"That man," Susie teased. "Just wait till he gets back. I'll give him an earful."

"I heard something through the grapevine, Susie; maybe you can confirm it for me?"

"Shoot."

"Rumor has it some Confederate bodies were found on the battlefield this morning. . . ." Ed let the question hang.

"Well, your grapevine is pretty good, Ed. We got a note this morning telling us there was a partially uncovered common grave with five Confederates buried in it at The Wheatfield. It went on to name the Confederates, including their rank, unit, and next of kin."

"You've got to be kidding," Ed stammered.

"Pretty amazing, huh?"

"Is it for real? The names, I mean?"

"We've already checked our files and confirmed that all five were here at Gettysburg, with Anderson's Brigade out of Georgia. All of them were reported either missing or killed. Warren thinks it's the genuine article, all right."

"But how could anyone know that?"

Susie shrugged invisibly on the other end of the phone. "How could anyone know exactly where to dig for them after so many years?" she countered.

"Well," Ed said, feeling a little dazed, "tell Warren I called. I'll give him a buzz this evening."

"Okay, Sugar. Bye."

"See ya." Ed set the receiver back in its cradle and stared blankly at the silent phone.

"Well?" Clair said. "What did she say?"

Ed looked up. "You were right. Five dead Confederates."

"Told ya," Clair said with a smile. "I gotta get back to work. Will ya stop by later?"

"Sure," Ed said, half-listening.

Running her hand across Ed's cheek in a subtle caress, Clair turned and slipped out the door.

Ed didn't watch her go. Propping his elbow on the counter, he let his fingers scratch absently at day-old stubble. "Who in the world would know where to dig for a bunch of old dead soldiers?" he mumbled to himself. Tossing this question around, a crazy thought entered his mind. But the more he thought about it, the less crazy it seemed.

"Andy, Andy, Andy," he muttered. "What are you into now?"

39

Monday, June 20

Richard Martin was excited. He was so excited that when he pulled into his driveway and leapt out of his 1984 Thunderbird, he left the engine idling and the door ajar. Halfway through the front door he realized what he had done. Slapping his forehead, he raced back to the car and shut the engine off. Retrieving his keys, he stuffed them in his front pocket and slammed the door.

"Andy? Get your camera," Richard blared, bolting through the front door and stampeding down the hallway like the bulls of Pamplona in search of daring Spaniards. "Alice? Hey, Alice?"

"Good grief, Richard! What is it?" Andy's mother said, stepping out of the kitchen with a dirty plate still in her hand.

"It's amazing," Dr. Martin said, fumbling for his glasses and rifling through the stack of books and papers piled high on the hallway credenza. "Where's my notebook?" Looking up, "Have you seen my notebook?"

"The blue one?"

"No. That's for class. The red one. The one with all the tabbed pages."

"I think you left it in the bedroom."

Racing up the stairs, he hollered, "Andy? You here?"

"He's at Jeff's," Alice called from the foot of the stairs. "Good grief, Richard, you're acting like a lunatic. Are you going to tell me what's going on?"

"Hang on," she heard Richard's muffled voice call from the end of the hall. A minute later he was back, storming down the stairs two at a time.

"Got it!" he said, holding the notebook high.

"For crying out loud, Richard, slow down! You're going to break your neck."

At the bottom of the stairs, Richard stopped and slapped his forehead with the palm of his hand. "The camera." Setting the notebook on the banister, he turned and was about to race back upstairs when Alice stopped him.

"Andy's camera is in the hall closet." Putting a calming hand on his chest, she said, "Just wait here and I'll get it."

"It's amazing, Alice," Richard stammered as his wife searched the hall closet. "Absolutely amazing."

"What is? I wish you'd just tell me. It's like you're possessed or something. I've never seen you like this."

"They found some bodies on the battlefield this morning."

"Murdered!" Alice gasped.

"No, no, no! Soldiers! Confederate soldiers according to the Rangers."

"Where?"

"Out at The Wheatfield."

Finding the camera, Alice closed the closet door and handed the 35mm to her husband. "Are you going to be able to get close enough to use that?" she asked.

"No problem," Richard beamed. "The Park Service called the college this morning and asked us to help record the site. Guess who's leading the project?"

But Alice knew the answer without guessing.

There was no one at Gettysburg College, probably no one in the entire state of Pennsylvania, more qualified to lead such an effort than Dr. Richard Martin.

"Congratulations!" she purred. "I guess this means you won't be home for dinner?"

Richard didn't answer. He just pecked her on the check, whispered, "I love you," in her ear, and disappeared out the door.

Alice stared at the closed door for a long moment. She listened to the car start and back out of the driveway, then shift into drive and race down the road.

She smiled, proud of her husband and the passion he held for his work. Starting back to the kitchen, she suddenly stopped and let out a little laugh. Picking up Richard's notebook from the banister, she opened the front door and waited on the steps for him to return.

That was Richard.

The perfect absent-minded professor.

40

News of dead soldiers – lost, then found – travels quickly through the media grapevine. Within this circle of journalists and pseudo-journalists there are those who have mastered the art of sensationalism. To these prize journalists, spotting a promising story comes as natural as cheating on your income tax.

Even when the story is still buried in the ground.

By Sunday afternoon the vultures of journalism were descending upon Gettysburg in force; and more were on the way. Earlier in the morning, a Gettysburg radio station dubbed the dead soldiers 'The Lost Confederates' and the title stuck like flies on a glue trap. By evening, news agencies in Tokyo, London, Paris, and Moscow were trumpeting the amazing discovery of 'The Lost Confederates'.

The world was captivated.

It wasn't the discovery itself that proved so sensational, but rather, the means of the discovery.

The note.

The partially exposed grave.

The mystery.

Who was responsible? How could anyone have known? Rumors flew wildly across radio and TV waves as networks hypothesized about the note-writer. The validity of the names scribbled on the note was challenged. How could anyone know the identity of five corpses lost for over a century? *Impossible*, the networks raged. It had to be a hoax.

Worse yet, no one could confirm that there were five bodies, since only one had been exposed by the mysterious note-writer. The National Park Service wisely refused to poke any further into the grave until a team of experts could examine the site. Until then, the media would have to wait and speculate.

And speculate they did.

On Monday, *CNN* spent an entire hour with a panel of experts trying to illustrate – with little success – how the discovery was simply the result of someone's personal research.

A mystery historian, they argued.

Someone with a passion for Gettysburg.

Perhaps a Civil War diary tipped off this mystery person to the common grave. Or a letter home from one of the soldiers who buried the Confederates. The possibilities were infinite, the experts argued. But they stressed that these possibilities absolutely, positively, excluded any supernatural connection.

Men of Science don't believe in the supernatural.

Men of Science believe only in Science.

On Friday, the *Inquisitor* printed a spectacular five-page spread on the discovery. Leading this bit of creative reporting was an exclusive interview with a psychic taxi driver from Philadelphia who claimed responsibility for the find.

Unlike Men of Science, yellow journalists will believe anything. Or, at the least, they hope their readers will.

41

Friday, July 15

At a quarter after eight, Ed managed to herd the last of his straggling customers out the front door of the Emporium, after flicking the lights on and off several times without success. Turning the deadbolt, he flipped the sign over to CLOSED. Staring at the crowded street outside, he muttered, "What a day!" then closed the blind.

The week was a busy one, with people flocking to Gettysburg from all over to see the Lost Confederates. The hotels were filled, the Bed and Breakfast Inns were packed, and a number of enterprising locals had decided to take in boarders. For a price, of course.

Like a crescendo, the fevered pitch of activity grew steadily throughout the week. Today was the busiest day of all, but Ed knew it would be nothing compared to Saturday and Sunday. The *chug-chug-chug* of the cash register gave a promising premonition of what the weekend would bring.

"Never seen so many tourists in all my years," Ed snorted, straightening a shelf of books before joining Andy behind the counter. "Good thing they only found five of those Confederates. I mean, I know they said the South would rise again, but I didn't think they'd come as tourists. For Pete's sake, I think the whole state of Virginia must be here and half of Georgia. Maybe if we dig up another regiment the rest of the Confederacy will just move on north."

Andy didn't respond, he just kept punching numbers into the adding machine on the counter. Leafing through the ones, fives, tens, and twenties stacked high in the register drawer, he looked at the total, then hit clear.

Counting the money a second time, he hit total and studied the paper printout as it spewed from the machine. Whistling softly, he looked up at Ed. "Looks like you hit the jackpot today."

"What?" Ed said, craning his neck. "Let me see that." Tearing off the paper printout, his eyes quickly tracked to the bottom line.

"Holy cow!"

"You grossed over thirty-two hundred dollars today," Andy said, confirming the figure on the printout in case Mr. Williams doubted his eyes.

"Thirty-two hundred fifty-seven dollars and twenty-eight cents," Ed said. Setting the paper on the counter, he looked at Andy in disbelief. "I've never grossed more than twelve hundred dollars in a single day in my entire life – even on my best days."

Slowly, a grin of realization crept over Ed's face. "Well, damn!" he hooted. "Looks like it's time to buy that wide-screen Panasonic I've had my eye on. We can watch *Home Improvement* in style."

Crumpling the paper into a ball, he tossed it across the room, trying to score a three-pointer off the poster bin next to the door. "Hallelujah!" he whooped. Then, raising a fist in the air, he shouted, "God bless the Confederate States of America!"

By eight-thirty the Civil War Emporium was buttoned up for the night. "How about an ice cream sundae up the street?" Ed offered. "My treat."

Wincing, Andy said, "I can't. I told Matt I'd be over at his place by nine."

"Oh," Ed said, nodding his understanding and trying to hide his disappointment.

"It's just that his dad has the night shift and the guys are coming over to watch movies. We rented *Cliffhanger* and some horror movie. I don't remember what it's called."

"Maybe tomorrow night then," Ed said.

"Sure."

Pausing at the front door, Andy turned and looked at Mr. Williams. "Why don't you come with me? We're gonna get some chips and dip and pig out. Just have some fun, you know?"

Mr. Williams shook his head. "Thanks for the offer, but I think tomorrow's gonna be a bear. I better get some sleep." Reaching into his pocket, Ed pulled out a twenty, walked over, and pressed it into Andy's hand. "Here, chips are on me."

"I can't take this!" Andy said, trying to give the bill back.

"Like hell! Take it! You've been here since noon. Where else am I gonna find someone who'll work for two bucks an hour?"

Andy hesitated, then pocketed the money. "All right. But this is for tomorrow too."

Ed brightened at this. "You gonna stop by and give me a hand tomorrow?"

"Sure," Andy grinned. "Where else ya gonna find someone who'll work for two bucks an hour?" Unlocking the door, he waved a good-bye. "See ya in the morning."

Then he was gone.

Locking the door, Ed watched him go with a sad smile. Walking back to the counter, he stared at the stack of money in the register drawer. "Thirty-two hundred dollars," he whistled. "Man, oh man."

Reaching under the counter, his hand fished around blindly for the bottle of Russian vodka he kept hidden. Touching cool glass, he wrapped his fingers around the neck of the bottle and pulled it clear. Pouring himself a shot, he tossed it down, then cringed as the liquor hit his taste buds.

Ed Williams wasn't much of a drinker, a vice he avoided for good reason. His father was an alcoholic, back in the days when they weren't called alcoholics.

They were drunks.

Booze-breathed, sinful drunks who couldn't control their lust for liquor. But that was before the medical profession found the disease hidden in the bottle. Nowadays they weren't called drunks. They were just booze-breathed, sinful alcoholics. That was Ed's special reason for avoiding the drink.

For two years the vodka bottle lay hidden under the counter, cracked open only on special occasions. Still it was half full. He might be a drunk's son, but Ed Williams would never be called a drunk.

Leaning on the counter, his mind wandered to Andy and the Marauders, and for a moment he was tempted to grab his keys and join them. After all, he was one of them, wasn't he? He was one of the boys. Didn't they always call him their pal? And wasn't he the one they came to when they needed advice?

He was at the front door unlocking the deadbolt before he stopped himself.

"You old fool," he muttered. "Where ya going? You're not a boy anymore." Locking the deadbolt again, he stared out at the busy street and remembered a time when he was thirteen.

But that was a long time ago — and a world away.

42

Saturday, July 16
Gettysburg Pak-N-Pay

Pushing a shopping cart through a grocery store on a Saturday afternoon is as close as you can come to a demolition derby without carbon monoxide. Similar steering maneuvers can be applied to both situations. There's the *fake-right-and-go-left* tactic to outwit a charging opponent; the *brake-and-reverse* tactic to avoid a head-on collision with the Formula One shopping cart that whips around the corner without warning; and, of course, there's the *nitrous oxide superboost* tactic to escape the debilitating effect of screaming kids.

Navigating through this mess like the novice he was, Jeff stopped his cart next to the chips and dip. He and Matt were on a shopping expedition; a quick trip that was turning out to be more complicated than either of them expected. Who knew there would be so many choices? So many people? Didn't they have anything better to do on a Saturday? It was mind-numbing.

The Pak-N-Pay sold every kind of chip imaginable – more than imaginable. There were the basics: the Doritos, Tostitos, and all the copycat brands. Then there were the traditional chips like Ruffles; chips that had been around for decades – and some tasted like it.

Jeff's eyes flitted over the brand names, making a mental inventory before choosing. "What do you think?"

"Do we really need chips?" Matt asked, curling his nose.

"Sure! . . . Yeah! What's a cookout without chips and dip?"

"You ever hear of cholesterol?"

"Ah, that's for old people."

"All right! Just grab a bag of Tostitos."

"Doritos are better."

"They're the same thing!"

"No they're not!" Jeff argued. "Doritos are crunchier."

Throwing his hands up, Matt said, "Whatever! Grab a bag of Doritos and let's go!"

"Better get two bags," Jeff said. "There's gonna be a lot of us. Well . . . maybe three bags."

Pushing Jeff aside, Matt grabbed three bags off the shelf and threw them into the cart. "Let's go!"

"Geez, switch to decaf," Jeff muttered, following Matt to the back of the store where the meat coolers were. Lining the rear wall, the coolers offered up a culinary delight of veal cutlets, sausage, prime rib, round-eye steak, hamburger, lean hamburger, ground turkey that looked like hamburger, and dozens of other cuts.

Matt stopped next to the pork section. "Here," he said, reaching into the cooler for two packages of pork chops and tossing them into the cart.

"Ewww! Why pork chops?" Jeff whined.

"I like pork chops."

"But they give you trilobites. Didn't you know that?"

"What?"

"They give you trilobites. Mrs. Jeffers told us last year in biology. They're little insects that eat your flesh when they get inside you."

"Trilobites are extinct, you fool! They're fossils!"

"Uh-uh! Mrs. Jeffers said you get them from eating pork."

"That's trichinosis, and it's caused by a parasite. Geez, you're so dense sometimes."

"Am not!"

"Are so!"

"Well, I still don't want some parasite eating my flesh."

"They don't eat your flesh."

"Uh-huh! It's like that germ that eats peoples' faces. It was on TV! I saw it!"

"What are you talking about?"

"My dad was watching it. Over in England they had this germ that got into people and it ate their flesh. Like some space alien or something. And then they have to amputate your arms and legs or you die."

"You're an idiot!"

"Hey! That's not nice," Jeff said, looking at Matt sheepishly — as if expecting an apology.

"It's true!" Matt shot back. "That was some rare virus, or something. I remember seeing a news show about it, probably the same one you saw. That doesn't have anything to do with trichinosis."

Looking at the pork chops with apprehension, Jeff said, "So, we won't get trilobites?"

"Trichinosis!"

"That's what I said!"

"No!" Matt replied, trying to calm himself. "As long as we cook them good, we won't get trichinosis."

151

Jeff smiled. "Okay." Looking up the aisle, his eyes suddenly lit up. "Hey! Let's get some hot dogs!" And off he trotted, fondling every hot dog package on the shelf as he *oohed* and *aahed*.

"What are you doing?" Matt demanded.

"Making sure they're fresh, Stupe!" Jeff shot back.

Matt just stared at him in disbelief. "How did I get talked into this?" he muttered to himself. But there was no time for such questions. It was time to grab a package of hot dogs and go.

Jeff was starting to draw a crowd.

43

Little Round Top
That Night

"**I**t's called a marshmallow," Grant explained to Abraham as he speared one of the small white pillows of goo on the tip of a metal roasting stick. "First ya roast your marshmallow until it starts to bubble – at least, that's the way I like 'em. Ya gotta be careful, though. If it gets too gooey it'll fall off the stick and into the fire."

Placing the marshmallow over the crackling flame, Grant handed the end of the stick to Abraham. Holding the stick out as if a deadly viper was writhing at the other end, Abraham looked apprehensive. "Like this?"

"A little closer," Grant said, grabbing the shaft of the roasting stick and pulling it toward the fire. "You'll be sitting here a long time if you hold it that far way. No. Now you're too close." Taking hold of the stick again, Grant positioned it a foot above the dancing flame.

"There," he said. "That's perfect. Not too close, not too far."

"The belly side is starting to bubble!" Abraham said.

"That's all right. That's what it's supposed to do. Turn it over. You want to keep turning it so that the whole thing gets evenly roasted."

"Like this?"

"Right. That's good."

Reaching into the bag at his side, Grant retrieved two small items that would prove to be of the utmost importance. Holding the first in his hand and extending it for Abraham's perusal, he said, "This is a graham cracker, and this," he said, holding up the second item, "is a square of chocolate."

Breaking the graham cracker in two and placing the chocolate on one half, he held his hand out. "Okay. Bring the end of the stick over here so the marshmallow is right over the chocolate."

Gently, Abraham swung the stick around.

"Hold it there," Grant said.

With the other half of the graham cracker on top of the marshmallow, he coaxed Abraham to pull out the roasting stick. This done, he squeezed down on the bubbling marshmallow, pressing it between the graham crackers.

"Voil`a!" Grant pronounced proudly. "What you have before you is a graham cracker, chocolate, and marshmallow sandwich. We call it a S'mores, cause you always want some more."

Snickering, he elbowed Abraham. "Get it? S'mores. Some more." Handing the sandwich to his Union friend, Grant said, "Go ahead, chomp away."

Abraham looked at the little sandwich suspiciously, sniffing at it like a dog might sniff at a wayward turtle. Licking cautiously at the dripping mix of marshmallow and chocolate, his eyes lit up and his mouth was suddenly emboldened.

Biting off half the sandwich, Abraham's eyes rolled to the back of his head and his vocal cords emitted an involuntary moan of ecstasy as he chewed. His throat trembled gently as he swallowed. Wolfing down the rest of the petite sandwich, he licked his sticky fingers until the nails started to show signs of wear.

"That was wonderful," Abraham sighed. "Could we have some more?" His words sounded more like a plea than a request. One hundred and thirty-one years of eating hardtack for breakfast, lunch, and dinner will do that to a fellow.

"I've got a whole bag of 'mallows, a box of crackers, and eight candy bars," Grant said with a devilish grin. "Far as I'm concerned, it's pig city."

Grabbing the end of Abraham's roasting stick, he fixed another marshmallow in place.

* * *

While Grant instructed Abraham in the art of S'mores roasting, Andy was standing at attention a dozen yards in front of them. With his drum hanging at his side, his hands began to tap out a simple tune Josh had just taught him. It was a lively beat meant for marching. A spirit-lifting *brump-bump-ump-ump* that Andy was starting to get into.

Beating out the last cords as if he'd been playing all his life, he finished the march with a roll and then the woods fell silent. Rising to the occasion, the half-dozen soldiers gathered nearby began to clap and hoot.

"You're much better, you know," Josh stated. "Much better."

Andy just grinned. "How 'bout one more?"

* * *

On the ridge, Matt and Jeff were learning the fine art of artillery. Their weapon of choice was a 12-pounder Napoleon; a model 1857. The gun's Chief of Piece, a sergeant by the name of Jenkins, was to be their instructor. He was a crusty old cannoneer who lived and breathed guns. Big guns, little guns, it didn't matter to Jenkins.

The smell of spent powder was his perfume.

The roar of cannon, his symphony.

Sergeant Jenkins loved his guns like few artillerymen could.

"Ya got four basic types of amm'nition for the 12-pounder," Jenkins lectured as he walked around to one of two ammunition chests on the caisson. "Ya got your solid shot, your shell, your spherical case, and your canister. They all have a diff'rent purpose and all work pretty good, but my favorite is the canister. 'Cause when those gray-bellies let loose with one of those Rebel yells and start in on ya, the old canister'll blow holes in their line like you ne'er seen. Lay 'em flat. Hell, I seen a dozen men blasted

154

deader than old Stonewall Jackson by a good canister shot. If ya got good cannoneers working the piece, you can get off maybe four canisters a minute. And that's a mighty deadly rate of fire."

Pulling a fixed round of canister from the ammunition chest, Jenkins tore off the paper bag covering the cartridge and handed the round to Matt. " 'Member what I showed ya now," Jenkins said. "I'll do the calling, you do the loading."

Matt nodded, then positioned himself across from Jeff at the front of the gun.

"Sponge!" Jenkins barked.

Jeff dipped the woolen end of the sponge rammer in a bucket of water at his feet and stuffed it down the barrel. He gave the sponge two turns while making sure he pressed firmly against the bottom of the bore.

Sponging, while helping to cool the barrel, served the dual purpose of extinguishing any embers left in the barrel from previous shots, thus preventing a premature detonation of the powder cartridge.

"Load!" Jenkins ordered.

Sliding the canister round into the barrel, Matt stepped clear as Jeff used the wooden end of the sponge rammer to ram the round home. At the rear of the piece, Sergeant Jenkins held his gloved thumb over the firing vent. This forced the air in the barrel to vent around the canister and out the front of the barrel.

Neglecting to seal the firing vent would allow air to rush out the rear of the gun as the round was rammed home. Like a bellow stimulating smoldering coals, this rushing air could breathe life back into dying embers in the barrel – even after a good sponging.

The result would be a deadly premature explosion.

Sighting down the barrel, Jenkins barked, "Train right!"

Running around to the rear of the piece, Matt grabbed the trail handspike on the carriage stock. Lifting the stock a few inches off the ground, he swung the carriage to the right.

"There!" Jenkins shouted, raising his hand.

Pricking the powder cartridge through the firing vent at the rear of the barrel, Jenkins hooked the lanyard – the trigger device – to the primer. Placing the primer in the vent he covered it with his left hand and moved to the rear.

"Ready boys?" Jenkins grinned.

Matt and Jeff nodded as they stepped apprehensively away from the loaded gun. Winking, Jenkins stepped clear of the wheel and pulled the lanyard.

KA-BOOM!

"Oooo-weee!" Jenkins hooted as a cloud of smoke and fire belched from the gun. "That was a nice one. Listen! Can ya hear it?"

"What?" Matt asked.

"The shot. Twenty-seven cast-iron balls in that canister. Can't ya hear them bouncing off the rocks at Devil's Den?"

But try as they might, neither Matt nor Jeff could hear the bouncing of Jenkins' shot as it rattled around the craggy fortress of rock below. Their ears were still ringing from the boom.

Rising from a deep crevice at Devil's Den, a lone Confederate soldier took aim with his musket and popped a shot in their direction.

Snorting, Jenkins said, "Don't suppose we disturbed him, do ya?" Then he laughed hysterically.

After cackling until he was starting to wheeze, Jenkins wiped his sleeve across his mouth and looked at the boys. "Don't suppose you got any of them pork chops left, huh?"

"Sorry," Matt replied. "They went pretty quick."

"How 'bout some of them hot beefs?"

"Beef hot dogs," Jeff corrected. "I think there's a couple left. Want me to see?"

"I'd be obliged."

As Jeff scurried off toward the campfire, Jenkins winked at Matt. "Don't get meat out here, ya know? Not even squirrel. Guess they all go straight to heaven. 'Cept for the horses. It's like they's stuck here with us. Like they sinned, too, and have to pay for it."

"Well, I wouldn't exactly call a hot dog meat," Matt said.

"What'cha mean?"

"Never mind. I'll tell you about it when you're done eating."

Jenkins placed the sponge rammer back through its holding loops on the side of the gun.

"Hot dog," he mused. "Why they call it such a silly thing anyhow? Aw!" he said suddenly. "It ain't made o' dog, is it?"

Matt laughed. "No! It's real beef."

Jenkins let out a sigh. "Good! Don't know if I could eat a dog. Ate a cat once, but don't know if I could eat a dog. 'Fraid it would remind me too much of my hunting dogs if I did."

Unknown to the eyes and ears of the Union army, Confederate troops were massing south of Devil's Den, out of sight of Little Round Top. Within the hour they would attack, pouring around Big Round Top like water around a timeless river boulder, making their way up the wooded southern slope of Little Round Top.

Jenkins would die in the attack.

His caisson, loaded with shot, shell, case, and canister, would be struck by a Confederate shell. The secondary explosion would destroy both Jenkins and his precious 12-pounder.

No one would cry, though.

Jenkins would be back.

In the morning everything would be back.

Morning always made things right.

44

Wednesday, August 3

Groundhogs are worth a quarter in Littlestown. Two dimes and a nickel and no one complains because it's okay to kill groundhogs in Littlestown.

In other parts of Pennsylvania, Puxutawney for example, where Groundhog Day is a big annual event, the slaughter of these burrowing mammals would have been looked upon with disdain and horror.

But in Littlestown, no one objects.

And since no one objects, that makes it all right with Grandpa Holtz. Twenty-five cents a head is what he pays his delinquent grandson to shoot the varmints. Twenty-five cents for every groundhog Burke skewered with his scoped twenty-two rifle.

"They're a damn nuisance," Grandpa Holtz fumed as he nursed a bottle of Jack Daniels stuffed inside a brown paper bag. "Nothing but overgrown rats, is what they is. Diggin' their burrows all under my barn. I got a cow, last week, broke his damn leg falling through one of them burrows. Had to shoot the poor bastard right 'tween the eyes; put it out of its misery."

Twenty-five cents a head.

A quarter.

In Burke's mind, that was a pretty fair price for popping overgrown rats. Leaning up against the wooden rail of a deteriorated fence, he sighted down range, waiting for a little head to stick up out of its burrow.

They couldn't stay down there forever, he assured himself. Groundhogs are active primarily during the day, so if they want to eat, they have to risk the gun.

Blam!

Risk the bullet.

Blam!

Burke liked killing groundhogs; he reveled in it. Even if his grandfather wasn't paying him to pop the little buggers, he'd gladly do it for free.

Just to kill something.

Blam! Blam! Blam!

Burke Holtz was the National Rifle Association's worst nightmare.

45

Friday, August 12

Midnight had come and gone when Andy saw the evil emerge from its dark lair. Sitting and talking quietly with Matt at the crest of Little Round Top, he saw the blackness seep silently from the woods and flow down toward Devil's Den like the slow motion dance of water cascading down a rocky riverbed. Andy could feel the hate and loathing. He could feel the evil intent of the entity.

Grabbing Matt and pointing, he said, "Do you see it?"

"See what?"

"The fog!"

A puzzled look crossed Matt's face. "Of course I see it. It's all over the place, you can't help seeing it."

Andy shook his head violently. "I'm not talking about the mist. I'm talking about the fog! The black fog! Right down there!"

Matt looked again, then slowly shook his head. "I don't see a black fog, Andy. Just the mist. There's no such thing as a black fog."

Evil was creeping into the trenches at Devil's Den now, whirling around the Confederates and their soft conversation as they sat before their fires.

"We'll have to go in a minute," Andy stated soberly. "They'll be coming." Strangely, as if someone had whispered in his ear, Andy suddenly knew the secret of the fog. Knew it as clearly as spring knows rain. The fog had always been here. Even before the war and the slaughter that coaxed it from its slumber. It now fed hatred to men who had forgotten how to forgive.

But why could he see it when the others couldn't?

Why couldn't the soldiers see they were being deceived?

These questions were naked for want of answers, answers that would have to wait. The Rebels were rising from the rocks at Devil's Den now, rushing up the slope of Little Round Top with the black fog waving over them like an unholy battle flag of enmity. Grabbing Andy by the shoulder, Matt said, "Time to go!"

Andy would never see the fog again, but it was there. He could feel its presence. Eternal as the rocks themselves, it was always nearby.

Waiting.

Watching.

Loathing.

46

The ceremony started at two o'clock in Lincoln Square, playing to a crowd of thousands. It was the largest gathering ever witnessed by Gettysburg, even dwarfing the popular reenactment that occupied the first days of every July.

They came from all over: buses, cars and campers from the surrounding counties, from Baltimore, New York, even Seattle and Los Angeles. Today was a special day for Civil War buffs. A day that would not likely repeat itself — ever.

The press arrived early, hovering over the crowd like vultures over ripe carrion. Asking ridiculous questions of passers-by in a vain attempt to fill dead air time before the ceremony began. Stuffed shirts with fake hair, pontificating on the historical significance of such an event. Today they were learned historians; tomorrow they would forget Gettysburg and don the hat of political analyst, biologist, social worker, or whatever cause was hot. Hypocrisy runs deep when truth is subject to ratings.

A Confederate fife and drum corps was the first to enter Lincoln Square, marching in slowly from the north along Carlisle Street to a sad funeral dirge that haunted the minds of those within earshot. Behind the fife and drum corps marched a full brigade of Confederates – re-enactors pulled from a dozen local regiments. Rifles shouldered, they stepped smartly yet solemnly, as if the music had already taken its toll upon their collective soul. Finally, the horse-drawn caissons rolled slowly by with their precious, flag-shrouded cargoes.

Five caissons for five caskets.

They were simple caskets, crafted of yellow pine and built in a style common to 1863. Matt Morgan, owner of Morgan Millworks on Hanover Road, volunteered to build the set of caskets at cost. With the help of his two sons, he proudly took to his task with the enthusiasm and reverence of a master craftsman who still believed in the Confederacy.

Into the lid of each casket he carved *Confederate States of America* along with the name of the man inside. Under this was carved *Anderson's Brigade* followed by the three-pillared Georgian coat of arms.

It was a fitting tribute.

Circling once around Lincoln Square for the sake of the crowd, the procession turned and headed down Baltimore Street. Twenty minutes later they arrived at National Cemetery, entering through the main gate on Baltimore Pike.

Andy, Matt, Jeff, and Grant watched the slow procession from a distance, knowing full well that, without them, none of this would be happening. They watched as the caissons stopped in the heart of the cemetery. Watched as the governor, several congressmen, and a number of other prominent figures served as pallbearers, setting the caskets to rest aside freshly turned soil.

They watched as the Confederate flags were removed from the caskets, one by one, and neatly folded into triangles by a Confederate Honor Guard.

And they watched as Confederate cannoneers loaded and fired seven 12-pounder Napoleons, booming out a twenty-one-gun salute that was heard as far away as Westminster, Maryland.

Beneath a tree a dozen yards from the burial site, silent and unseen by mortal eyes, five Confederate soldiers watched the proceedings with curious eyes. Rarely were they allowed to see into the mortal world, but today was special.

Leaning on his rifle, Sergeant Benjamin Moser watched as his body was lowered into the ground. In all his years of fighting on the fields and hills of Gettysburg, the old soldier had learned a great deal about death and dying; about pain and suffering.

He was hard.

He was a warrior.

After dying a thousand deaths you no longer cry out in pain when the bullet hits you, you just bite your lip until the blood flows and crumple to the ground. No one sheds a tear for you because they know in the morning you'll rise again to fight the battle once more.

Forever fighting.

Forever dying.

But now, perhaps things were changing; at least for Benjamin. Watching his body go into the ground to the silent prayers of the tens of thousands who stood and paid homage, the hardened warrior began to soften.

Bowing his head, Benjamin sobbed softly, his chest rising and falling in an exaggerated manner as he fought to control himself. But the battle was already lost. A tear trickled down his cheek, followed by another, and then another.

Good tears.

Healing tears.

Tears of solace and joy.

"We are not forgotten," he wept.

Throwing his weapon to the ground and looking to the sky, Benjamin Moser fell to his knees and in a humble and sorrowful voice, he cried, "Lord, I'm ready to come home."

In a flash of light more brilliant than a thousand suns, Ben vanished, carried to Heaven on a beam of sunlight.

Seeing this awesome display, the other four Rebels quickly tossed their weapons aside and, on bent knees, called on God to take them as well. Praying for all they were worth to end the nightmare.

The sky rumbled.

The clouds parted.

Shooting down from the heavens, a second flash of light struck the men. When it passed, Confederate Privates George McCoy, Andrew Day, William Hall, and Thaddeus Strafford were gone.

For them as well, the battle was over.

Those who gathered to witness the burial that day would remember how a cloudy day suddenly turned brilliant. How the air was light and alive; filled with energy. They would remember how the sun broke free of the clouds just as the caskets were being lowered into the ground. They would remember the brilliant rays of light that pierced the clouds and shot down to earth, lighting up a nearby tree in radiant sunlight. They would remember a distant rumble that sounded like thunder but wasn't.

They would remember.

47

Fort Apache
Tuesday, August 16

"**O**kay, here's the deal," Jeff said, standing next to an old towel tacked to the wall of the fort. "We need a good luck symbol, or gesture, or whatever you call it. And I had an idea last night." He paused, as if the gravity of the moment demanded a slow presentation.

Andy, Matt, and Grant just stared at him in patient annoyance.

"Under this towel is our new symbol," Jeff continued, obviously pleased with himself. "My dad and I were watching one of those World War II submarine movies last night, *Hell-Fire Cats of the Pacific*, or something like that. No! *Thirty Seconds Under Tokyo.*"

"You dork," Matt laughed. "It's *Thirty Seconds Over Tokyo*, and it's about airplanes, not submarines."

"No," Jeff insisted, not quite understanding, "It was about submarines."

Looking at Andy, Matt muttered, "I give up. You try."

"Forget it," Andy said.

"Can I finish please?" Jeff snapped, somewhat indignant.

When quiet prevailed, he tapped the towel and continued. "On the submarine, whenever they'd go to battle stations, they'd run out of their sleeping area–"

"Berthing," Andy said.

"Okay, they'd run out of their berthing area and on the wall was this picture of one of those pin-up girls. For luck, they'd pat her on the butt. So I had an idea. I thought we could put a pin-up girl next to our door so that whenever we leave we can pat her for luck."

"He *is* twisted," Matt said to Andy. Then, turning to Jeff, "Did you think of that all by yourself?"

"I'm not going to pat no picture girl's butt," Grant whined.

"Come on you guys. We need a good luck symbol." Lifting the towel, Jeff pleaded, "See, I got my best poster."

Tacked to the wall was a blowup of Geena Davis in a thong swimsuit – cheek out.

"See, we just give her a little pat right here," Jeff said, touching Geena's exposed cheek gently, as if it might explode if he pressed too hard.

"He is twisted," Matt said with finality. "You've been staring at too many of those naked women in your dad's girlie magazines. Besides, if I'm gonna pat someone's cheek, I want the real thing."

Looking at Andy and Grant, he said, "Who's got Geena's phone number? Someone give Geena a call. Tell her she's got three normal guys and a pervert who want to touch her butt."

Andy and Grant laughed.

Jeff stewed. "Very funny," he said, dropping the towel. "I thought it was a good idea. I thought you boneheads would like it. I guess I was wrong."

Flopping down on the couch, he stared angrily at the floor.

"Okay, all right," Andy said, seeing that Jeff was truly hurt. Holding his hand up, he quieted Matt and Grant. "Maybe Jeff's right. We could all use a little luck. I vote we give Geena a little pat whenever we leave the fort. Who seconds?"

Matt smirked at first, then, reluctantly, he said, "All right, I second the motion."

"Okay," Grant said. "I'll pat her cheek, too. Just as long as Jeff promises not to slobber all over it."

"Not funny," Jeff said, though he was obviously pleased with the turnaround.

Standing, Matt bowed low to the picture. "Welcome to Fort Apache, Ma'am," he said. "Would you like your right cheek fondled, or your left?" Laughing wildly and contagiously, like boys are wont to do, they each walked over and took a turn patting the picture.

"Just like sailors," Jeff beamed.

When it was over, even Geena was still smiling.

48

Little Round Top
Monday, August 22

George Fallow was from Boise, Idaho. A recently retired school teacher, George wasn't much of an out-of-state traveler. He preferred camping the rivers, lakes, and mountains of his native state. In sixty-three years, he had been out of Idaho exactly four times.

There was the trip to Vegas in 1972 – he didn't care much for the gambling – and three visits with his sister, Rose, in Eugene, Oregon. In 1984 he almost went to Yellowstone National Park, but his camper broke an axle twenty miles outside of Boise and he was forced to turn back.

Now he was at Gettysburg.

After forty years teaching history, this was about as real as it would get for George. He was never much for the Civil War, per se, but that was now changing. Standing at the crest of Little Round Top and visualizing the fierce battle that took place below, George Fallow found himself wishing he had known Gettysburg before now.

He wished he had known his new friend before now, too. A boy with a gleam in his eye that spoke of his passion for history. A boy by the name of Andrew Martin.

Andy was busy pointing out the different monuments and explaining the events of the three-day battle to George as the old school teacher looked on in amazement. His amazement was not so much over the events of the battle, but over his young guide's enthusiasm. *Where were such young scholars when I was teaching?* he asked himself.

But now it was getting late and Andy had to start home. They exchanged addresses and shook hands, saying cordial good-byes and wishing each other the best. They were friends. Once met, but friends nonetheless.

Passion is often the potting soil for a rose we call friendship.

Andy had such passion. And, thanks to a twelve-year old historian, so did George Fallow.

49

Dinner was always at five o'clock at the Martin home. Five o'clock sharp. No excuses. No exceptions. Looking quickly at his watch as he pedaled furiously up Taneytown Road, Andy realized he wasn't going to make it.

It was already ten after.

In his mind he could see the look on his father's face as he walked through the door. It was never a condemning look, just a disappointed one. Professor Martin expected the same promptness from his children as he did his students. "Life is hard on the unreliable," Richard Martin often said.

There was never any punishment, not unless he was very late, and that never happened. But those eyes, that disappointed stare; that was punishment enough for a boy who loved his father.

Pedaling harder, Andy crossed Steinwehr over to South Washington Street. Without realizing it, he reached up and felt for the paper in his shirt pocket. A folded paper that held the scribbled address of a house in Boise, Idaho.

A house Andy would never visit.

Past the hospital he turned onto Breckenridge. Two more blocks and he'd be home.

"Well, well. Look who it is," Burke Holtz sneered, elbowing Pete Krump, one of his pint-sized henchmen. "It's Martin. The little butt-head who poisoned me a couple months ago."

Protruding from Burke's hand was a black leather leash; attached to the other end of the leash was Pogo.

Pogo was a dog.

A big dog.

Part Labrador, part Bull Mastiff.

By his appearance, one was led to believe that Pogo favored his Bull Mastiff genes. Standing two and a half feet at the shoulders and dressed in a bulky coat of rippling muscles, he looked far less than Lassie-friendly.

Andy was racing toward Burke and in his rush he didn't immediately recognize his foe. When the distance between them closed to a block, Burke unfastened the leash from Pogo's collar, saying, "Go get him, boy!"

At a furious pace, Pogo homed in on Andy and closed for the kill, barking viciously as he came.

"What if he bites him?" Pete said, a trace of worry in his cracking voice.

"Na," Burke replied in ignorant bliss. "Pogo doesn't bite, he just barks like a sum-bitch."

Andy spotted the charging dog when it was almost too late. Instinctively, he reached for the shampoo gun, wrestling it from its holster with his left hand. As he did so, his grip on the handlebar slipped and it jerked sharply to the right.

Instantly, the bike darted off the sidewalk and into the street. Dropping the gun, Andy reached for the handlebar to steady himself, but it was too late.

At thirty-five miles an hour, the driver of the Buick Regal had no time to react. He hit Andy head-on and bounced him up into the windshield.

The glass shattered.

Ten thousand pebble-like fragments.

One for every dream that died on the hood of that car.

In an instant Andy was gone, rolling up the windshield and over the roof as the driver of the car slammed on his brakes. The squeal of stubborn tires against the pavement echoed a terrible scream of doom off the houses lining the street. Then there was silence. A silence that grew . . . and grew . . . and grew.

Eerily and lasting.

A throbbing silence that filled the neighborhood for a moment's eternity until people started pouring out their front doors, running to see what had happened. People who had lived on Breckenridge all their lives. Neighbors who watched Andy grow up, who paid him to mow their lawns or weed their gardens. Neighbors who bought chocolate bars from him to support the school computer club.

This wasn't *their* Andy lying in the street.

Not Andy Martin!

It had to be a mistake!

But as they approached, grandmothers suddenly wailed in anguish and mothers covered their faces in weeping hands.

It *was* their Andy.

It couldn't be.

Shouldn't be.

But still it was.

He lay motionless in a crumpled heap at the center of the street, a small pool of blood growing around him and draining slowly off into the gutter at the side of the road. A trickling stream of life's fluids stolen from a boy who was not yet finished using them.

Running toward him, their anguish growing, the neighbors shouted chaotically at one another to call an ambulance, to get some blankets. They shouted anything that would enforce the illusion that there was still something they could do to save Andy.

But there wasn't.

He was fallen.

Slain by the God of Technology and the Demon of Ignorance; the drummer had fallen.

In three weeks he would have turned thirteen.

50

Saturday, August 27
Evergreen Cemetery

On the southern fringe of Gettysburg, nestled on a serene hill, Evergreen Cemetery was founded in the year 1855. It was a quiet cemetery with a sweeping view of the lowlands. Peaceful and imposing. What better purpose for such a hill than to give rest to the dead.

From the cemetery's ornate gatehouse a ridge ran south, parallel to Taneytown Road, ending at Little Round Top. This was Cemetery Ridge. It was upon this rise that Union forces placed their hopes during the three-day battle. If they could hold the high ground, victory would surely greet them. Failure to do so would be devastating. Thus, for a brief moment in history, the occupants of Evergreen Cemetery were roused by the rumble of cannon and the blast of musketry.

Called to reveille by bugle, fife, and drum.

During the battle that followed, some of the headstones were damaged. Trampled by careless soldiers or chipped and broken by errant minie´ balls. Windows in the two-story gatehouse were shot out and the soil around the cemetery was disturbed as U.S. artillery batteries dug in and built their earthworks. It was a disgrace, but no one worried about such things during war. There would be time to worry later.

The Union came first.

Save the Union, the dead will wait.

No one said it, but many thought it.

The dignity of the dead would be restored after the last charge. Until then, the living took precedence over their fallen ancestors. Besides, more dead would soon be lying exposed on the blood-soaked fields of Gettysburg than were resting in Evergreen Cemetery. Who would worry for their dignity?

Bodies bloating in the hot July sun.

Trampled fields choking on precious blood.

Several months after the fighting moved on to other quarters, leaving the dead behind in their shallow graves, Gettysburg National Cemetery was established. Situated on a seventeen-acre parcel of land purchased in the name of Pennsylvania for the sum of $2,475.87, National Cemetery played neighbor to its elder kin, Evergreen Cemetery. Only a fence separated the two.

Once again, the hill knew tranquility.

Jove knows what man thou might'st have made;
but I, thou diedst, a most rare boy . . .

Cymbeline
—William Shakespeare

Andy would be buried at Evergreen Cemetery, to rest forever above the battlefields he loved so dearly. Ironically, his plot was only seventy yards from that of the Lost Confederates.

That would have pleased him.

The funeral service was short, with pews packed full and people standing in the aisles and at the back of the church. It was a quiet service, broken only by the silent weeping of those who came to say good-bye. And though the sermon was beautiful, few actually heard the words. Stricken by grief, they stared instead into empty space, as if looking for the face of a boy who no longer was. It's hard when the young die. Hard on those left behind.

It is the death of a thousand dreams.

A shattered hope.

It was the death of a father's dream that one day his son would be a prominent historian, lecturing and writing books. Feeding his passion to a world that often cared little for the lessons that history offers.

It was a shattered hope for the mother who looked forward to growing old bathed in the love of a devoted son.

She now clutched only a memory.

Today they buried a son.

But they also buried a dream.

A love.

A hope.

Such black days fall on those who can bear them the least.

Following the service, Andy's white casket was carried to the hearse and ushered silently to Evergreen Cemetery.

Here would be the final good-bye, but not for Matt.

Rising weakly from his seat, he fell to the floor of the church, weeping uncontrollably, calling Andy's name in the tortured voice of one whose soul has been ripped asunder. Calling to one who could no longer answer. Gently, Steve Jacobs picked his boy up and cradled him in his arms. With tears streaming down his face, he turned and carried Matt home.

At the cemetery, Reverend Holling said some final words; words meant to comfort and assure. Words that, no matter how well spoken, seemed to ring hollow in the ears of the bereaved. The Reverend survived most of the service without a tear, but now, near the end, the grief was beginning to take its toll. This was a boy he knew and loved, not a stranger or an infrequent acquaintance. Speaking from a portable pulpit next to the casket, Reverend Holling faltered and then stopped. Taking his glasses off, he pulled a handkerchief from the inside pocket of his suit and wiped his eyes dry. Folding his glasses and sliding them into his breast pocket, he ended with the only five words he could utter. Five words everyone knew to be true, but needed to hear anyway.

"He was a good boy," the Reverend cried quietly.

He was a good boy.

One by one, family, friends, and neighbors came forward to pay their last respects. April May stepped quietly to the side of the casket, her eyes swollen from crying and her mascara streaked and running. In her hand she held a single red rose; a sweetheart rose.

"Good-bye, little boyfriend," she whispered through her tears. Laying the rose gently at the foot of the casket, she wept softly. "I'm going to miss you," she whispered. Bowing her head, she turned and walked away, knowing that a piece of her heart would be buried this day.

Mr. Williams waited until the Reverend and only a handful of others were present before stepping forward to say his good-byes. For him, this was one of the hardest days he had ever faced. Today he buried a boy who was like a son; like a grandson. A boy who, in the end, was his dearest friend.

Standing next to the casket, Ed reached into his pocket and pulled out a small rectangular box. Fumbling with the clasp, he managed to open the lid, despite fingers made clumsy by grief. Gently, he extracted the Silver Star medal he had earned so many years before.

"I want you to have this, Andy," he choked, laying the medal at the head of the casket. "Thanks for being the best friend a tired old man could ask for." Tears teased the corners of his sorrowful eyes, but he contained himself.

He would cry, but later. In his own time.

Right now he had to be strong for Richard, Alice, and Brett.

"I'm empty, Andy," Ed said, patting the casket softly. "I feel like someone's stolen my soul. I'm so tired."

Putting the empty box back in his pocket, Ed Williams turned and walked slowly from the cemetery. At the front gate he paused and looked back.

"I'll never forget you, little buddy," he whispered.

And he never would.

51

Monday, August 29

Richard Martin looked much older than his forty-four years when he walked through the door of the Civil War Emporium. The small bell over the door announced his arrival at the same moment the old wall clock began to sing its top of the hour song.

It was eight o'clock.

Ed looked up from the register and forced a smile as Richard walked the short distance from the door. In Richard's hand was Andy's drum.

"I was never really very good at this," Ed said, his voice tired and hollow. "The money I mean. I was never very good at closing out the register. That's why he'd always come by to help me close. He never said it, but he knew I wasn't good with numbers. That kid," he said, shaking his head, his voice trailing off. "He said he just liked talking to me."

Staring at the counter top and fingering the register receipt,

Ed realized that this was no time to deal with his own sorrow. "How's Alice?" he asked.

Richard nodded. "Better," he said. "She insisted on going to work today. Probably better that way. Get her thinking about other things. If she stays in the house she'll just sit in his room and cry."

There were tears in Richard's eyes now, welling up and trickling down his cheeks; but his voice was still steady. Setting the drum on the counter, he said, "I wanted to return this to you. I know you gave it to Andy, but I think he'd want you to have it back."

His voice was starting to break now.

"He thought very highly of you, Ed. You know my father died when Andy was only three, and Alice's father lives in Houston."

Ed nodded, his head hanging low.

"Andy never really had a grandfather – not one that was close. Then he met you, and . . ." Richard covered his eyes with a clumsy hand, wiping the tears away. "Thank you, Ed. That's all I wanted to say. Andy loved you like a grandfather."

Turning, he made his way to the door and was gone before Ed could say a word. Picking the drum up, Ed turned it over in his hands slowly, lost in thought, lost in sorrow. Walking to the back corner of the store, he put it back on the shelf where it had sat for so long before. At the front door he flipped the sign over to CLOSED and locked the deadbolt.

Back behind the counter he tried closing out the register again but couldn't. His vision blurred as tears welled up in his eyes and streamed down his cheeks. Dropping the receipts and burying his head in his arms, Mr. Williams began to sob; his tears soon growing into a wail of anguish that begins in the soul and shakes the entire body.

There is no pain like that of the soul.

For the second time in forty years, Ed Williams wept. It would be the last time tears stained his face. Within two years the bacon and eggs would catch up with him and he would join Andy in Evergreen Cemetery. On his marker would be a simple epitaph: Carpe Diem!

Seize the day!

52

Friday, September 2

Friday evening was always a busy time at the Emporium. Between four and five in the afternoon newly arrived tourists would start making their first rounds, shop by shop. With a treasure hunter's eye they searched for something special, something unique. They didn't know what. Somewhere in one of the town's many shops they were sure to find it, though. Stashed away on a shelf in some obscure corner they would find the T-shirt, the spoon, or the mug that they knew they couldn't do without. Back at home they would display their prize on a shelf or in a cabinet; further defining themselves by the clutter they built their dreams upon.

It was this unpious quest for useless trinkets that had pushed Ed toward the austere life he now led. "I'm a minimalist," he once explained. "Less clutter a happy home doth make." He didn't mind selling that clutter to others, though.

Pushing open the Emporium's door, Matt was surprised to find the store nearly empty. Then he realized what time it was and strolled over to the counter. Looking up from the register, Ed smiled warmly as he pulled his glasses off and shoved them carelessly into his shirt pocket.

"What brings you out tonight, Master Jacobs?" Ed asked.

"Just thought I'd stop by. You closing?"

"In a couple minutes," Ed said, glancing absently at the old wall clock.

"What you doing tonight?"

"Well, I don't have a hot date, if that's what you mean. Why?" Before Matt could answer, Ed winked and leaned close. "Gonna treat me to a movie and some popcorn?"

Matt broke into a wide smile and was surprised at how good it felt – almost refreshing. "Me and Jeff and Grant were gonna do something tonight, but it's a secret. We were wondering if you wanted to come, but you got to remember not to tell no one."

Mr. Williams frowned. "Last time you boys had a big secret it was because you were seeing ghosts. Remember that?"

Matt didn't answer.

"This isn't more ghosts, is it?" Ed asked, growing suspicious at Matt's silence. "It is, isn't it?"

Matt picked at an imaginary spot on the counter. "Sort of," he said softly. "Andy wanted to show you a while ago, but we didn't think it was a good idea."

"Does this have anything to do with the Lost Confederates?"

Matt looked up now and locked eyes with Mr. Williams. "Yes. In a way it does."

Ed eased himself down in his chair and pushed himself back against the wall as he exhaled deeply. Scratching at the stubble on his chin he eyed Matt, studying his face and his nervous hands. "Okay," he said at last. "What do I have to do? You want me to meet you someplace or are you gonna stop by and get me?"

Matt was smiling again. "We'll stop by . . . around eleven."

Ed grimaced. "A little late, isn't it? Remember, this is Labor Day weekend. I got to be up early. Mentally sharp and all that. There's gonna be a lot of people here tomorrow – and on through Monday."

"Sorry. It's gotta be late. Any earlier would be too risky."

Shrugging, Ed said, "You're the boss. If I'm blurry-eyed tomorrow, I'll know who to blame. Just have to suck down a couple extra cups of Clair's coffee."

Pushing himself off the wall, Ed leaned on the counter and looked directly at Matt with a penetrating stare. "Ya know, I have to admit that I'm intrigued."

"Intrigued?"

"Yeah, I suspected you and Andy had something to do with those Confederates all along. Not exactly something you come out and ask someone, though. Leastwise, not if you want to keep them as friends. People might think you're a little tetched if you were to ask them if they've found any dead Confederate soldiers lately. Know what I mean?"

Matt smiled and nodded.

"Eleven o'clock then," Mr. Williams said.

"We'll stop by and pick you up."

175

Matt was almost to the door when a thought struck him. "Do you have a bike?" he asked over his shoulder.

Ed nodded. "Haven't ridden it in years, though."

"You're gonna need it."

"No problem. I'll have to check the tires, though. Long as we don't go on no *Tour de France* I should be all right."

"We'll go slow," Matt grinned.

"I'm not that old," Ed shot back.

"See ya at eleven." With a wave of his hand, Matt was gone.

"Looks like I'm gonna miss Letterman," Ed mused. As if on cue, the old wall clock chimed its eight bells and it was time to close.

Time to find a tire pump.

53

Stars play brightly on moonless nights. When the moon warms its pockmarked face in the golden rays of another continent's sun, leaving the midnight sky over Gettysburg untended, the stars play ever so brightly. Scorning their master for his absence, they sparkle and glimmer with a new found fire that beckons the Icarus in every man.

Tonight, Icarus wears the clothes of a man named Williams. A simple old man who lacks the wings of his aerial muse but embraces the spirit nonetheless. In silence he stares into the sky and drinks the night's ale, sipping it slowly through admiring eyes. Knowing that God gave a gift to Pennsylvania when He painted stars in their sky.

The whir of thin tires on asphalt soon disturbed this serenity as the Marauders stormed the Emporium at full speed, screeching to a shuddering halt in front of its proprietor.

Ed just shook his head. "Well, boys, where to?"

"Little Round Top," Matt answered.

Ed nodded, his eyes reflecting the stars. "What are we going to find there? Can you give me a hint, or are you going to spring it on me all at once?"

"You wouldn't believe us if we told you," Jeff said.

Matt nodded slowly. "He's right. If we tried explaining it to you, we'd just mess it up and you'd think we were crazy or something. We've got to show you. Then you'll understand."

Ed shrugged. "Okay. If that's the way it's got to be, that's the way it's got to be." Waving his hand at the battlefield, he said, "Lead on."

They rode in silence, enjoying the crisp air. The last couple of days were unusually cool for Pennsylvania at this time of year, a welcome change from the sultry days of summer. The weather forecast promised a magnificent Labor Day weekend, the best in years.

After a brisk ride that was all too long for Mr. Williams, they pulled into the parking lot at the crest of Little Round Top. With whispered words of caution, the boys led Mr. Williams off the asphalt and up a trail. Stopping next to an outcropping of rock, they stashed the bikes, then proceeded through the trees in search of a tent they hoped would still be there.

It was.

A black hole in the night.

As it loomed before them, Ed halted. "What the—? . . . What's this tent doing up here? Did you boys do this?"

"Not us," Matt answered. "It's been here. It's always been here; you just can't see it most of the time."

"Would you mind explaining that to me?" Ed said. "'Cause frankly, boys, I'm getting a little nervous."

"We're going into the tent," Matt said. "We want you to follow us. Believe me, it's worth it. It'll answer some of your questions and give you a whole bunch more to ask."

"What's in there?"

Matt stepped close to Ed, close enough to read his features. "You'll have to trust me," he said. "But I promise you, if you don't believe in ghosts now, you will in a few minutes."

Ed grimaced, as if facing an unpleasant task. "All right," he sighed, "I'll follow. Much as this place gives me the creeps, I'll follow."

Matt smiled, then stepped through the tent flap. Turning, he winked. "See you on the other side."

Then he was gone.

"You better go next, Mr. Williams," Jeff said, pushing the old man forward. "Me and Grant will bring up the rear."

Nodding nervously, Ed shuffled closer to the tent. Sticking his head through the flap and peering around the dark interior, he muttered, "What have I gotten myself into?" Rubbing his hands together and taking a deep breath, he resigned himself to the will of the tent. Closing his eyes and holding his breath, he stepped through the opening.

He was flying now, pulled forward by the tent's vacuum and sucked through the tunnel. As he flew, a peace fell over Ed and he smiled. For a moment he was Icarus. Brave, bold Icarus flying toward the sun.

Then, just as quickly as it began, the ride ended.

With the foggy mind of one waking from slumber, he felt a hand around his arm, pulling him from the tent. "That wasn't bad, now was it?" Matt said, leading him clear of the portal just as Jeff and Grant popped through.

"Wow! Look how light it is," Ed said, his eyes scanning the sky. "What happened? How come everything's so light?"

"We're in the spirit world now," Matt answered.

Ed snorted. "You're gonna have to do better than that!"

Before Matt could say more there was a rustling nearby. A moment later, Josh and Major Prichard appeared.

Ed's jaw dropped.

Jogging down the path, Josh and the major stopped dead in their tracks and Prichard started for his revolver before they recognized their friends.

"Matt, Jeff, Grant!" Josh said. "I was starting to wonder if you gave us up. I kept coming to the tent, day after day, but you were never here."

"You're fortunate we happened by," Major Prichard added. "We were just on our way to check the pickets. Care to join us?"

Stopping suddenly, he looked Ed up and down. "Who's this? And where's Andy?"

"Mr. Williams," Matt said, "I'd like you to meet Josh Harding and Major Jonathan Prichard."

"My pleasure, Sir," Major Prichard beamed.

"So this is Mr. Williams," Josh said. "He looks different from my impression of him. 'Spected him to look like old General Lee, I suppose. Proper and with a beard. Gentlemanly." Extending his hand to Ed, he smiled. "A pleasure to make your acquaintance."

"Nice to meet you," Ed muttered, a dazed look in his eyes.

"Where's Andy?" Josh pressed.

Matt dropped his eyes and hoped someone else would answer, but it wasn't to be. Taking a deep breath, he exhaled hard words. "He's dead."

Josh and Major Prichard exchanged looks of disbelief. "How did it happen?" Prichard asked after a moment.

"He got hit by a car."

"A car?"

"It's like a carriage that propels itself," Matt explained.

With a nod, Josh said, "I've seen them before. During the day, when the people come, they ride in iron carriages."

Prichard knew Josh could see into the mortal world from time to time and understood immediately what he meant. "When did this happen?"

"Almost two weeks ago," Matt answered.

Matt, Jeff and Grant took turns telling Josh and Major Prichard about the accident and the funeral. When they finished, they consoled themselves and each other, as friends do at such times. Mr. Williams watched this exchange in fascinated silence, staring at Josh and Major Prichard like a blind man who sees for the first time.

For two weeks a black weight had been bearing down on the old proprietor's soul. An oppressive, crushing weight of loss and sorrow. But now, as he listened, this weight seemed to lessen. He didn't know why. Couldn't explain how. It just did.

Mr. Williams, the eternal skeptic, never claimed to have witnessed a miracle in his life. Miracles were for the faithful and those who clung to hope. He had no use for such things. But as his young friends stood talking with the spirits of soldiers dead and buried for over a century, he knew that something was happening.

Something powerful.

A miracle.

Stepping forward and lifting his eyes to the trees, Ed studied the forest about him with his head cocked to one side as if listening. "Can you feel it?" he muttered.

"Did you say something?" Matt asked.

"Can you feel it?" Ed now cried. "The air. It's electric."

As he spoke, a powerful blast of warm air emanated from the woods to the east. It carried the subtle scent of sweet flowers and the promise of tranquility.

This was no Pennsylvania wind.

In the trees beyond the parking lot a small light appeared. No bigger than a lantern at first, it mushroomed quickly, growing larger with each passing second until it swallowed the parking lot in a glow like none they had ever seen.

"What is this?" Prichard said in a startled voice. "A Confederate trick?"

"No!" Mr. Williams said, his face beaming as he surged past them and pointed excitedly. "Can't you see? Can't you see the angels?"

But to Matt and the others there were no angels. Just light. Light more powerful than any they had ever seen. A radiant blast of white energy that seemed to burrow through their eyes and into their minds – into their souls. As they stared into the light's brilliant white center, something moved.

At the core of the light there was movement.

A small mass.

Unrecognizable.

A shadow against the brilliant field of white.

They stared transfixed, eyes glued to the tiny dot as it grew larger. It was approaching them, they could see that now. As if from a great distance, the shadow glided slowly toward them. They saw it with the vision of the nearsighted.

Discernible, yet indiscernible.

A figure without form.

An unrecognizable shape.

As it moved closer it began to come into focus. Clearer with every passing second. Focusing now. Drawing closer, until at last they could see the form; the head, arms, torso, and legs. Still they did not know if it was man, angel, or God.

Regardless, it was coming.

At the edge of the light the figure paused, then stepped free of the brilliant white glow. Gliding gracefully toward them, the being seemed to carry part of the great light in its bosom, casting shadows among the trees as it moved.

"It *is* an angel," Matt gasped.

He would soon discover how wrong he was. Matt and the others, despite their many visits to the spirit world, still knew few of its secrets. Until now, they had never seen a spirit of light or glimpsed Heaven's gate. If they had, perhaps they would have known what the angels know. Perhaps they would have known that there are beings in the afterworld far greater than angels. Selfless spirits so pure they command the respect and admiration of all God's creatures. To these beings the angels bow low and sing eternal praise.

Tonight, such a spirit walked among the dead at Gettysburg.

Mr. Williams was the first to recognize the heavenly visitor. As he stumbled toward the spirit of light with outstretched arms, his lips parted and he cried, "Andy!"

So it was.

Walking toward them gracefully, as if gliding, Andy smiled at his friends and the glow that surrounded him brightened. Stopping before them, his radiance seemed to reach out and envelope his mortal friends. Andy greeted them with dancing eyes that knew only joy, embracing each of them in turn. Then he spoke, and though his voice was his own, it somehow seemed wiser and more at peace – almost divine. "Follow me," he said. "You will want to see this."

Without waiting for a response he turned and started down the southwest slope of Little Round Top. Matt and the others didn't ask themselves why? or how could this be? They just followed.

In ones and twos, Union and Confederate soldiers stepped from behind their breastworks to stare at the spirit of light descending the hill. Silently, they watched the radiant spirit make his way toward Devil's Den. Without knowing why, they began to follow. Rising from their fortifications, the Union troops trudged down the hill, keeping their eyes on the spirit and taking little

181

notice of the rough terrain. At Devil's Den, the Confederates laid down their arms and let the enemy come. Somehow the battle didn't seem important now.

No shot was fired.

No cannon roared.

All was silent as Andy ascended the rocky slope around Devil's Den, climbing slowly to the flat top of the highest boulder. Like Moses at Sinai, he stood on high and looked down at tortured souls yearning for peace. Standing on the rock and shimmering against the backdrop of night, Andy was a beacon for all the world to see. Raising his arms, he motioned the souls of the dead forward.

No one resisted.

From the woods and from the hills they came, the spirits of the damned. Men who knew only battle; spirits who knew only hate and revenge. They gathered at the base of the rock, Union and Confederate, side by side. When their number approached a thousand, a hush fell over them, as if by some silent command.

Then Andy spoke.

He spoke words no mortal can hear. Words of comfort and hope, words that Matt, Jeff, Grant, and Ed would not remember the next day. There are things that mortal minds cannot conceive of or comprehend without facing madness. It is of such things that Andy spoke.

He talked of wounds unhealed. Of spirits adrift in their own enmity, riding a storm-tossed sea of hate. He spoke of a great nation that rose from the ashes of the Civil War and freed the world from tyranny in the following century.

He spoke of the incredible power of love and forgiveness.

Finally, he spoke of Heaven.

When he finished, the crowd remained silent except for those who had fallen to the ground weeping. Slowly, Andy descended the rock, looking into the eyes of the men below him as he came. Looking into their souls to see if he had reached them.

Stepping from the rock, men fell on him in an embrace of tears and sorrow, reaching for him with arms that longed for rest. Throwing their weapons aside, mighty warriors crumbled to their knees by the hundreds, begging God's forgiveness and praying for deliverance from the Hell they had cast themselves into.

Raising his arm and pointing to the top of the boulder, Andy spoke loudly so that all could hear. "Heaven," he sang, "is but a step away for those who will surrender their hate." A brilliant flash burst overhead as the top of the boulder was drenched in radiant light.

Heaven's light.

"Take me!" men wailed as they surged forward. En masse they scrabbled up the boulder and into the light, their arms outstretched as if to embrace loved ones long sought and dearly missed. Nine hundred souls climbed the rock that night. Nine hundred weeping and weary souls embraced the light.

Major Prichard made his way up the rock.

As did Josh.

But not before a long and sentimental round of good-byes.

"I'll see you on the other side, my friends," Josh promised when only he and Andy remained. "When it's your turn, Andy and I will be waiting for you."

Climbing the rock slowly, he paused at the top and looked down. "I'll not forget you," Josh shouted. "Don't you forget me."

With a smile, he stepped into the light. For a moment they could see the look on his face turn to ecstasy before he vanished in the warm glow.

Josh was home.

Only Andy remained. Stepping close to his friends, he embraced each in turn. "I must be going soon," he said.

"To Heaven?" Ed asked.

"Yes."

"It's real, then? Heaven is real?"

"It is the only thing that is real," Andy replied. "It is the living who trudge through shadows and obscurity. Your world is but an echo of Heaven, you must remember that. And if you ever doubt Heaven's existence, ask yourself this: which is more real, the shadow, or that which casts the shadow? Which rings more clearly, the echo or the shout? In your answer you will find your faith."

"Does-" Matt paused. "Does everyone go to Heaven?"

Andy shook his head sadly.

"My mom?"

"She is there," Andy smiled. "She is a wonderful spirit of joy

- so radiant. She's always laughing. I've enjoyed her company greatly."

Matt struggled with a flood of emotions as these words sank in. "Can you–" his words dropped off as the tears burst from his eyes. Breathing deeply in gasps, he steadied himself. "Would you tell her I love her? I don't remember ever telling her."

Andy stepped close to his dear friend and embraced him again. Putting his mouth to Matt's ear, he whispered, "Why don't you tell her yourself." Without another word, Andy pointed to the top of the boulder. As he did, a figure stepped from the light. A radiant young woman who looked down into Matt's eyes and saw a part of her own soul.

"Mom!" Matt wailed, tears streaming down his face.

Rushing recklessly up the face of the boulder he flew into his mother's arms and their tears mingled as they held one another. Tightly they clung to one another, an embrace to make up for the life together that they had lost .

As mother and child sank to the ground embraced, weeping tears of joy, music that none of them could hear began to play several miles away. It was the tune of an old music box playing of its own accord. Playing *It's a Small World After All* under a young boy's bed.

Andy walked with his friends that night, walked in the fields and around the rocks they shared on so many nights. On their backs they stared at the stars one last time until Andy said the words that none of them wished to hear.

"I must be going."

They embraced him again at the base of the boulder, each holding him and not wanting to let go, until all of them were holding him at once. A cluster of friends so close and so rare.

There were no tears as he climbed the rock.

Only joy.

Andy was still with them.

In spirit, he would always be with them.

At the top of the boulder he turned and smiled, his eyes sparkling like stars. With a wave, he mouthed a final 'Good-bye' and stepped into the shimmering white glow of Heaven.

Staring after him, the Marauders could see angels in the light; smiling beings of joy and happiness. As the light began to fade, the sounds of Heaven drifted down to them. Instruments and

184

voices rising together in songs of such beauty that one note would slay the mortal body of man.

A moment later Devil's Den faded into darkness and silence as the light winked out. Matt, Ed, Jeff and Grant sat for a long while on the rocks that night. No words were spoken between them, they just sat. Sometimes smiling, sometimes crying, but in the end, healing. When they started back to town in the early morning hours, Matt paused for a brief moment as the others rode ahead.

Looking out over the battlefield, he began to realize the true significance of the night's events. He had witnessed the redemption of souls – souls by the hundreds. The terrible wound hacked into the collective soul of Gettysburg so many years before was beginning to heal. The past was the past.

The Battle of Gettysburg was over.

54

Saturday, September 3

It was 2:00 a.m. exactly when Matt sat up in bed and glanced around his room. His mind was troubled by a dream that seemed all too real. As if he were an observer, he saw himself standing next to the tent with Josh. Battle raged on the slope below and as he watched, a riderless horse broke free of the melee and raced toward them. The dream was eerily silent so Matt didn't hear the report of the musket, but he saw the puff of smoke in the nearby woods and watched in horror as the horse went down almost on top of them. The wounded animal thrashed about wildly, rolling on top of the tent and smashing it to the ground before regaining its feet and staggering off into the woods to die. Then, in his otherwise silent dream, Matt heard a loud boom, like a drum, and woke with a start.

Looking out his half-shaded window, Matt suddenly knew what the dream meant. Dressing quickly, he tiptoed downstairs and out the back door. A few minutes later he was in Jeff's backyard, pelting his friend's window with acorns. After several well-placed shots struck the glass, Jeff's groggy face peered out. Rubbing the sleep from his eyes, he unlatched the window and pushed it open.

Matt explained the purpose of his visit twice before Jeff's sleepy brain could grasp it. Reluctantly, he agreed to get dressed and come down. Even half-asleep, Jeff knew he had little choice.

Grant was next. Fortunately, he proved easier to arouse, mostly because his bedroom window was at ground level. Nothing will wake a boy faster from a sound sleep then someone rapping at the window he's sleeping under. This is usually a symptom of too many horror movies. When you're twelve or thirteen, you still haven't figured out that the wolfman doesn't knock before entering.

Ditching the bikes among the boulders at Little Round Top, the Marauders made their way to that dark portal that was now so familiar. But tonight the tent was gone. All that greeted them was a stand of trees and the rustle of deer grazing nearby. Looking about, Matt, Jeff, and Grant realized how empty the woods seemed without the tent.

"Give me the shovel," Matt said.

Using the blade like a pick, he broke the hard packed surface in an outline roughly the shape of the missing tent. Scooping out the soil inside this rectangle, Matt only had to dig a few inches before running into resistance. "See? I told ya so!" he said, tapping excitedly at the loose dirt.

Dropping to their knees, Jeff and Grant started digging with their bare hands. They were eager and hopeful now that the riddle was close to being solved. In a moment they would know. They would have an answer to the question that still chased their imaginations on quiet nights.

"Careful you don't cut yourselves," Matt cautioned. Setting the shovel aside, he dropped down next to Jeff and clawed at the soil. A moment later, Matt knew that he was right. With the hooded flashlight, he lit up the hole.

The glimmer of metal greeted him.

The golden shimmer of a brass drum.

Josh's drum.

It was crushed flat, as if something heavy had fallen on it – a horse, if Matt's dream was correct. Wiping away the dirt and grime with a towel from his knapsack, Matt suddenly grew excited. "Look! Here!" he said as he tapped the upper edge of the crushed instrument.

Etched into the brass lip in fancy scroll was the confirmation they were looking for.

Josh H.

It was a brass drum that once had few equals. Now, as Matt looked upon it for the first time, a voice echoed down to him from what seemed like a thousand years before. A voice that whispered, "I've lost m'drum," from across the boundaries of time.

Forty-five minutes later, Matt said good night to Jeff and Grant and started for home. As he turned off Breckenridge onto West Street, he coasted to a stop in front of the Martin house. A light was on in Andy's room. Without knowing why, Matt eased his bike quietly to the sidewalk and sat down on the little stone bench Mrs. Martin had placed in the flower bed by the road. "We found it, Andy," he whispered to the night. "We found the drum."

Tilting his head back, he gazed longingly at the stars. Slowly, his eyes fell down across the ceiling of night and finally came to rest back on Andy's window. He could picture Alice Martin sitting sadly on her son's bed, perhaps crying, perhaps too tired to cry. Matt felt pity for her. If he felt like dying after losing Andy, how much worse was it for her?

Oddly, the light in Andy's room was now moving, as if someone had picked up Andy's lamp and was carrying it toward the window. Stranger still, the lampshade shadows that should have graced the walls and ceiling were not there. Only uninterrupted light – pure light – as if from a naked bulb. A moment later Matt knew the truth. It wasn't Mrs. Martin after all. And it wasn't a lamp.

Stepping to the window in splendor and grace, a majestic angel smiled down at Matt. He was a spectacular being of light who radiated warmth and understanding. Matt had never heard of or seen an Angel of Comfort before, but as he looked on this wonderful being, he understood why the spirit was there.

Sorrow had paid a visit on the Martin home and the angel was there to see that comfort was now brought in equal measure. He would stay with the Martins until they overcame their loss. At night, when the nightmares came, the angel would whisper soft words of comfort that only the soul can hear.

In time, Richard, Alice, and Brett would begin to heal. They would be able to say Andy's name with a smile of sweet memory, rather than a tear of sorrow. Comforted, they would once again know peace. Taking what joy they could from a son they knew too briefly. With his job complete, the angel would finally leave the Martin home, but he would never stray far from their hearts.

In the summer of 1996 this same Angel of Comfort, whose name is unpronounceable to mankind, would greet the spirit of Mr. Williams as the old man's mortal remains crumpled to the floor of the Civil War Emporium. Embracing Ed's soul, the angel would carry him to an eternal reunion in a place no one grows tired of. A happy reunion with a boy called Andy – the best friend an old man could have.

Gettysburg Gazette

Monday, September 5, 1994

Park Rangers were greeted this morning by a mysterious note tacked to the door of the Cyclorama, the second such note in two months. This time, however, it came with a special package: a damaged Union drum.

According to sources at the Park Service, the note identifies the drum as belonging to Joshua Harding, a 15-year old drummer killed near Little Round Top. The note requests that the drum be buried with Mr. Harding because, "he's been looking for it."

Park officials have confirmed the authenticity of the drum but won't speculate on the source of the information contained in the note. Arrangements are being made to inter the drum at National Cemetery with its owner, Joshua Harding. A special ceremony is planned.

Epilogue

Time is a relentless beast, marching on despite the efforts of man; belonging to and controlled by none but God. Unlike the creations of man, time cannot be manipulated. There is no pause, like on the television remote. No frame-by-frame. No commercials that offer time to ponder substance and meaning.

Time simply is.

What is a hundred years? Is it nothing more than the wink of an angel's eye? Perhaps. And what happens after mortal time stops and the ghost leaves the body? More importantly, is there a ghost? These are the questions that boys ask as they grow into men. Even more so as men grow into old men.

The fate of Matt, Jeff, and Grant laid down this road. Yet with each passing summer they gather with steadfast loyalty at a place now sacred. Sacred because they have learned the meaning of life and have recognized it for what it is.

For three nights in July they gather at Devil's Den, lying on the cool rocks after the Park has closed, gazing upon the whirling mass of stars, moon, and planets. A brilliant blackness we call night.

Pulses quicken as ears strain against the sounds of the night. It will come. They know this with the certainty of tradition, yet they are eager for the thrill.

An hour passes, then two.

They wait.

Then, as if in the distance, it begins. Soft at first, barely audible. But soon the flutter grows stronger and the *brrump brrump brrump* of not one, but two drums can be heard. The phantom rhythm echoes off the rocks of Devil's Den as the men smile with closed eyes, their minds swaying to the beat. They can no longer see the spirits of their friends, but they know they are near. Only a breath and a world away.

As the drums play on, strummed by celestial hands, each man, in his mind and in his turn, ponders the frailty of life. The beat now sounds like a boisterous heart. Or is it their own hearts, pounding with excitement?

The thrill.

A heart beat and a drum beat, in chorus together. One from this world, one from beyond. In time, both will stop and one world will leap into the next. Such is life and death and life again. Such is the frailty of man.

These are special moments for the three, not filled with anxiety and dread, but peace and understanding. Precious moments. Soon, too soon, the drums begin to fade back into the darkness. They smile. Who cares if a sentimental tear of remembrance plays at the corner of an eye. They have shared tears before.

When it is over they stand and brush the dirt from one another's back in silence. Each afraid to speak for fear of destroying the magic. The lights of Gettysburg are shining brightly when they start back to town; to live life another year, until the next gathering. As they draw back into the reality of their own world, they console themselves with the knowledge that no matter where they may wander, in their hearts they are always together. For they are company to a great secret that few can conceive of or comprehend.

They know what happens . . . *when the drummer falls.*